Only One Bed

Also by Keira Andrews

Contemporary

Honeymoon for One
Beyond the Sea
Ends of the Earth
Arctic Fire
The Chimera Affair

Holiday
Only One Bed
Merry Cherry Christmas
The Christmas Deal
Santa Daddy
In Case of Emergency
Eight Nights in December
If Only in My Dreams
Where the Lovelight Gleams
Gay Romance Holiday Collection

Sports
Kiss and Cry
Reading the Signs
Cold War
The Next Competitor
Love Match
Synchronicity (free read!)

Gay Amish Romance Series
A Forbidden Rumspringa
A Clean Break
A Way Home
A Very English Christmas

Valor Duology
Valor on the Move
Test of Valor
Complete Valor Duology

Lifeguards of Barking Beach
Flash Rip
Swept Away (free read!)

Historical

Kidnapped by the Pirate
Semper Fi
The Station
Voyageurs (free read!)

Paranormal

Kick at the Darkness
Kick at the Darkness
Fight the Tide

Taste of Midnight (free read!)

Fantasy

Barbarian Duet
Wed to the Barbarian
The Barbarian's Vow

Only One Bed

KEIRA ANDREWS

Only One Bed
Written and published by Keira Andrews
Cover by Dar Albert
Formatting by BB eBooks

Copyright © 2021 by Keira Andrews

ISBN: 978-1-988260-73-0

Acknowledgments

My thanks to Leta Blake, Anara, Mary, and Rai for their encouragement and invaluable support in bringing this story to life and making it the best it can be.

Special thanks to Elizabeth for her insights on growing up Japanese Canadian.

I've been a skating fan for decades, and it's always a joy to write about the sport. Any similarities to real skaters and coaches is entirely unintentional and coincidental.

Chapter One

Sam

IF MY GRANDMA wasn't so cute, I'd tell her to bite me.

She beamed up at me with her crinkly grin, white hair peeking out from her red Team Canada toque. She wore her usual prim and proper outfit of slacks, blouse, and cardigan, her face fully made up—Yuko Tanaka did not leave the house without her rose-colored lipstick.

But every time we went to a skating competition, she proudly topped her outfit with the red woolen hat. I'm not especially tall, but she barely reached my shoulder, the hat's pom-pom giving her a few extra inches.

Her elbow struck just below my ribs as she asked again, "Where's your boyfriend?"

I rolled my eyes at her old joke as I stepped

back to let a woman pass through the concessions line. This was a brand-new arena in the Calgary burbs built for the Olympics in fourteen months, but there still wasn't enough room on the concourse. Never was. "You know Etienne's not my boyfriend. He's my best friend."

"Eh?"

I leaned down and repeated firmly, "You know Etienne's not my boyfriend."

"Why not?" Her brown eyes sparkled.

"Because I have a girlfriend. *Obaachan*, stop trolling."

Fine, I *used* to have a girlfriend. Though Mandy had nothing to do with why Etienne wasn't my boyfriend. I was straight. It was my older brother, Henry, who was gay. The end.

She *hmphed*. She loved this game of being unconvinced that Etienne and I weren't secretly on the down low. "Why isn't he here?" My grandma didn't follow skating results unless Henry was involved.

"Etienne and Brianna didn't make the Grand Prix Final. They're not at that level, remember?" I quickly added, "They're still having a great season! But only the top six teams from the Grand Prix events make it. They didn't medal at either of their competitions this fall."

They'd been fifteenth in ice dance at the last World Championships, which was amazing when you thought about it, but they weren't medal contenders internationally. They never got the scores they deserved, but the judging was so political and fucked-up.

"Mmm." Now her gaze turned critical. "What did you do to your beautiful hair?"

"Cut it." It was shaved close at the back and sides and longer on top. I'd spiked up the front with gel.

"Don't be a wise man."

"I'm not. No frankincense or myrrh on hand. Definitely no gold." I elbowed her arm gently. "Get it?"

She snorted. "Very good, Samu." She'd called me that for as long as I could remember.

"It'll wash out." I ran a hand over the tips of my hair that I'd highlighted a metallic silver-green in contrast to my natural near-black. "Eventually."

The pom-pom danced as she shook her head. "Your cousin Keiji in Osaka just got a big promotion. No green hair."

"Keiji's a banker. I'm in third year sociology at UBC. No one cares about my hair."

"No ripped pants either. You look like you're poor."

"There's nothing wrong with being poor. It's a social construct." Although my jeans had *not* been cheap. "I know, I know, no baggy hoodies for Keiji either. Or Henry." Between my perfect cousin and my uptight, extremely tidy brother, my grandma had a ton of comparison material. My mom said she'd done the same thing to her when she was growing up and to ignore it.

Hand snaking under my hoodie, she pinched my waist. She was still lightning fast. "You're a good boy anyway."

I lightly batted her pom-pom. "I love you too."

We reached the front of the line and ordered hot dogs, fries, and pretzels. The menu here had a Wild West theme, but aside from the chuckwagon chili, it was all the usual crap. I was an expert in arena food, and while the content of hot dogs was questionable at best, the pizza was never fresh and suffered more from sitting under warmers.

Obaachan insisted on carrying the tray of pop, already sucking on her Orange Crush. "It's Henry who really needs a boyfriend," she said.

"Shh!" Juggling the tray of food, I squirted ketchup into little white paper cups at the condiment stand.

I glanced at the people milling around. Between fans, families, friends, coaches, and media, skating was a small world and gossip was a main food group. Henry was a former world champion fighting for gold in singles against his arch nemesis from the States, Theo Sullivan. Everyone here knew who Henry was, and he would *not* appreciate Obaachan discussing his love life—or lack of it—

so loudly.

I mean, she wasn't wrong—Henry needed a boyfriend. Or at least to get laid. Not that I knew for sure he wasn't getting any. My big brother would discuss his real or nonexistent sex life with me right about *never in a million years*. I worried sometimes that he was lonely, but he was too obsessed with skating and beating Theo to date.

Etienne said *he* was too busy these days for a boyfriend too. I wasn't a world class athlete, and while I had enough to do between classes and my job re-shelving books at the library, I wasn't sure what my excuse was for not seeing anyone again since Mandy. It had only been a few months, though. I'd been happier playing League online with Etienne on weekends.

It was fine—I didn't have to party all the time to meet another girl. My buddies at school kept telling me about all the hot chicks they picked up with the latest app. I said I'd download it when I was back home in Vancouver in January. I'd be busy enough playing with Etienne anyway. We were really close to reaching the next level and couldn't stop now.

Obaachan and I shuffled to our section through a short concrete corridor and then down the steps. We were in the third row in the corner near the Kiss and Cry, and a family had to stand up to let us squeeze by to our seats. A dance mix of

"Last Christmas," which I hated yet knew all the words to, echoed through the arena as the Zamboni steadily cleaned the ice, leaving it shiny and smooth.

After handing off food to my parents, I tried to get comfortable. Seriously, who fit in arena seats? I was on the skinny side and only five-six, but my knees hit the chair in front of me. Obaachan and the kids under ten beside me were the only people who didn't look uncomfortable.

On my grandma's other side, Mom asked, "Sam, you're sure you only want money for Christmas?" She tapped her phone, frowning.

"Uh-huh. There's no point in having to carry stuff home."

It was mid-December, and we'd be heading to Toronto soon to spend Christmas there with Henry since there was no way he'd stop training for the holidays. He'd be forced to on the days the rink closed, but he was too obsessed to take an actual week off or something.

I missed the old days when Henry and Etienne both trained in Vancouver and I saw them anytime I wanted. I opened my texts, itching to send Etienne a message. But I shouldn't distract him when I didn't have anything specific to say. "*I miss you*" would just be weird.

After the judges and officials were introduced, which always took a stupidly long time, the overhead lights temporarily dimmed and thumping music played in time with strobes as the six women competing in singles skated to center ice for their introductions.

We applauded the lone American, two Japanese skaters, and three Russians. We didn't always attend all four disciplines when we went to Henry's competitions, but at the Grand Prix Final it was only the best and we had an all-event pass.

Just before the American girl began—but after the noise of applause had faded—Obaachan declared, "That dress makes her look like a stewardess."

Mom and I shushed her in unison. As a kid at one of Henry's competitions, I'd mercilessly roasted another skater who fell on half his jumps, even though my parents told me to lay off. Turned out that the skater's mom was sitting right behind us, which I only realized when he joined her later, his face all red and puffy from crying. His mom gave me the biggest stink eye, and I'd wanted to sink through the floor.

I'd hated being dragged to Henry's competitions back then, but the shame of being so *mean* had stuck with me. I'd grown to like skating way more over the years, especially after I became friends with Etienne in grade nine. I knew how much criticism skaters had to deal with from every direction.

Admittedly, Obaachan wasn't wrong about the dress—all that was missing was a scarf around her neck and a tray of drinks.

After the women's short program ended, there was another break before the men began. The Zamboni rumbled out again, and I chewed the ice from the bottom of my pop. The arena announcer told us there were surprise guests.

In the Kiss and Cry, the TV reporter who did the post-skate interviews got on the mic. A familiar couple stood beside her, their image flashing up on the scoreboard screen to thunderous applause.

Huh. What were Chloe Desjardins and Phillipe Vincent doing here? They'd reigned as the top Canadian ice dancers for years and had won three or four world championships. Maybe five? They had been pegged to win Olympic gold, but they fell on their twizzles in the rhythm dance—those quick spins on one foot in perfect unison were like the quads of ice dance. The Russians beat them.

They retired after that, so why were they in Calgary for the Grand Prix Final? Probably doing some charity thing or maybe fluff pieces for the network. Their outfits were too stylish to simply be attending the event. Chloe's lips shone her trademark pink, her golden curls perfect.

"You've got a big announcement today, don't you?" the reporter asked with a coy smile. Chloe and Phillipe looked equally coy. Even smug, which was weird. Maybe they had a new endorsement deal? They'd already gotten engaged, though they weren't married yet.

My stomach clenched. Oh fuck. No. Don't say it. *Do not say it.* Don't—

"That's right, Karen! We're coming out of retirement and competing next season!" Chloe exclaimed with a beaming smile.

Fuuuuuuck.

The audience lost its shit, cheering and clapping and probably tweeting the news already. Even my mom was clapping as Obaachan asked us to repeat what they'd said.

Mom answered, "Chloe and Phillipe are coming back!"

"Mom!" I hissed.

"What?" She blinked at my outrage in confusion. "That'll be nice for them. They really should have won gold in France."

"Not so nice for Etienne and Brianna!"

It took her a second before understanding dawned. "Ah. How many spots are there for us in ice dance?"

"Two for Worlds this year. I can't see them placing high enough to earn three for the Olympics."

My heart raced as I did the math. If Etienne and Brianna made it to Worlds this season, they and the other team—which would surely be the reigning champions, Anita Patel and Christopher Ferguson—would have to rank high enough that their placements added up to thirteen.

Anita and Chris had been sixth in the world last year. If they matched it, then Etienne and Brianna would have to be seventh. There was no way they'd jump up that high even if they skated their very best. Canada would only have two ice dance spots for the Olympics, and Etienne and Bree were screwed.

Fuuuuuuck.

I apologized to the family beside me as I leapt up and practically crawled over them to reach the aisle. The ice resurfacing would take a bit longer. They still had to introduce the men's judges since it was a different panel for each discipline, then the skaters would have their warmup. Henry was skating fifth, so with judging and replays, there was time.

I had to talk to Etienne.

After taking the stairs two at a time, I ducked outside through the first open glass door I could find since there were too many people around for privacy. In the fading light, a blast of frigid air slapped me, my fingers instantly numb as I pulled out my phone and tapped. Snowflakes swirled around me, the Rockies barely visible in the distance.

Etienne picked up the video call almost immediately, grinning into the camera. "Hey!" He looked like he was in the gym. Buds dangled from his ears, and a row of elliptical machines extended behind him, only one in use. He held up a bottle of disinfectant. "Just finishing the machines."

His brown hair was damp, and sweat glistened in the hollow of his throat, so he'd probably worked out recently. He and Bree were allowed to exercise for free at the private arena gym in exchange for cleaning.

It looked like he hadn't shaved in a few days, a shadow of stubble over his pale skin. His chest hair peeked out over the V-neck of his workout shirt.

"Um, hello?"

I realized I was staring and jerked back to attention. "Yes! Hi! How's it going?"

His mouth went tight, and he shrugged. "Okay. I mean, it's good. I'm good!"

Honestly, I thought Etienne was miserable in Hackensack. Yeah, he and Bree were training with the hottest coach in ice dance, but neither of them seemed happy. It bugged me that Etienne wouldn't admit it, but I didn't want to piss him off by pushing. It was like when my grandma still smoked. She had to get to that point herself where she wanted to make the change.

Etienne squinted. "Where are you?"

"Outside the arena." Shivering, I side-stepped until I was under one of the big lights coming on.

Snow was drifting, and I regretted only wearing Jordans. Not to mention only being in my hoodie.

"Your hair!"

"Oh, yeah." I swiped at the highlights. Maybe it *had* been a bad idea.

"I love it." Etienne flashed his perfect grin. He'd had his teeth fixed last year after a skating official mentioned it. I kind of missed his crooked canine. Not that I spent time thinking about my best friend's smile.

"Yeah?" I was weirdly relieved. "Cool. Thanks."

"Looks like it's snowing."

I brushed flakes from my head. "Yeah, a bit. Anyway, I just wanted to…" Shit. He clearly hadn't heard the news yet. How was I going to break it?

His thick eyebrows met. "What's up? Did Henry fall in the short?"

"No, he hasn't skated yet. I need to get back inside soon. The thing is…"

Etienne's frown deepened, his eyes flicking up and finger moving toward the screen. "Sorry, bunch of texts coming in."

There was the figure skating gossip machine exploding into action. I blurted, "Chloe and Phillipe are coming back!"

Etienne had lowered the phone to wipe a cloth over a weight bench, and he bolted upright, the phone jerking with him. He looked down into the camera, practically a nostril view.

"What?"

"They announced that they're returning to competition next season. They're here in Calgary, which is a big flex considering their top rivals are all in the building."

Etienne wiped his forehead. He breathed harder now. "They're coming back?"

I nodded. "I'm sorry. I know this is… I'm sorry."

"*Tabarnak!*" Though he spoke fluent English and only had a slight French accent, when he was upset, this classic Quebecois swear word was his go-to.

He closed his eyes, and yep, I could see right up his flaring nostrils from this angle. Then he was moving, and the camera showed the ceiling and walls, bouncing around. Etienne's heavy breathing was the only sound.

I hugged my free arm around myself, fidgeting and pulling up my hood as the dry wind gusted, hard snow peppering my cheeks. Etienne's face reappeared, creased and grim. It looked like he was in a gray bathroom stall now.

"I'm sorry," I repeated.

He nodded. "We thought maybe, but…"

"Is Bree there?"

His mouth tightened as he shook his head. "It

was a bad day for her."

Crap. She'd suffered a concussion months ago, and the effects were lingering way longer than anyone expected. "Do you think her phone is on?"

"Yeah, even though it shouldn't be. I need to get home."

Etienne and Brianna shared an apartment near their training rink in New Jersey. They got sick of each other sometimes, but skating was expensive AF.

"Okay. I should get inside. Henry's coming up."

Etienne nodded. "Hope he does great." He swallowed hard, Adam's apple bobbing. "Thanks for telling me. I guess we'll—I don't know." After a silence, he nodded again. "Thanks for telling me."

"Yeah, of course." I wanted to say something reassuring, but all that came out was, "Later." He gave me a tight smile and disconnected.

Teeth chattering, I ran to the closest entrance and joined the line. There were lots of exits and only a few doors letting people in. Because this day was trash, I realized I didn't have my ticket since my mom had them all on her phone.

Fuuuuuuck.

Chapter Two

Etienne

WHAT WAS THIS all for? What was the point if we didn't make the Olympics?

The drive to the apartment wasn't long, but it felt like forever before I stood in front of my door. Key out, I hesitated. Maybe Bree was sleeping. It was barely eight o'clock, but she needed the rest. Maybe she didn't know yet.

I didn't want to open the door. I wanted to keep living in this world where losing our Olympic spot wasn't real yet. Seeing Bree's face would make it official in a way that I didn't want to deal with. I stood there squeezing the key so hard the little jagged metal teeth dug into my skin.

After a deep breath, like the kind I took before a performance, I turned the key. The cramped living room was dark, and I flipped on the overhead light. Bree sat curled on the couch, and she threw up her hand over her eyes, wincing.

"Sorry, sorry," I murmured, keeping my voice low as I turned off the light and took off my running shoes and jacket. I blinked, waiting to adjust. The cheap plastic blinds were up, street-lights illuminating the saggy couch and armchair. If Bree had been feeling better, the TV probably would be on.

"So," she said.

"So." I slumped on the other end of the couch, feeling wearier than I should have since we hadn't been able to train today.

"I guess I can't blame them." Bree fiddled with the end of her messy ponytail. In the dim light from the street, her thick, honey-colored hair looked darker than usual. She had her long legs tucked beside her under a fuzzy throw blanket. Her sweatshirt sleeves hung low over her hands, the edges frayed.

I wanted to argue, but I only sighed. Chloe and Phillipe were a team that would end up in the hall of fame. Yeah, they wanted another shot at Olympic gold. I would too. "It still sucks."

"That it does." Not looking at me, she reached her left hand toward me across the couch. I took it automatically, squeezing her familiar palm. "People will say we're still young. We can stay in until the next Olympics."

I couldn't hold in a groan. It was true—in five years, we'd only be twenty-six. Definitely still young enough to compete in ice dance. But god, the thought of how much work it would be— grind, grind, grind—made me want to go to bed and pull the covers over my head.

Five more years of our parents spending every extra penny on our training. Five more years of injuries and treatment. Five more years of trying to be better and probably never being quite good enough.

Five more years until I could go back to piano.

I inhaled through the pang of longing. Some- times, I dreamed of playing again, and I woke with my fingers stroking imaginary keys. But there was no room in our shoebox apartment for a piano, and an electric keyboard wasn't the same. It only made me miss playing a real piano more. If I didn't have to work shifts at the arena snack bar as well as cleaning the gym, I'd have tried to find a teacher with a piano I could use.

Squeezing Bree's fingers, I said, "I guess we'll see how we feel."

"Yeah."

Silence stretched out, but it wasn't awkward. We'd agreed when we were paired up at fourteen that we'd go one season at a time. But of course with the Olympics in Calgary next season, we were going for it. There was a young team at our heels wanting that second spot in Canada, but it was ours to lose.

Except now Chloe and Phillipe would be number one. Anita and Chris would be number two. We'd probably be third, but it wouldn't matter if there were only two spots for the Olympic team. Getting three wasn't realistically going to happen.

"It's not fair." Bree whispered, her voice thick with tears.

I tugged her hand, and she moved across the couch, tucking against my side and under my arm. I kissed the top of her head. "It's not."

We both knew fairness had nothing to do with it. It was competition, and if two teams were better than us, that was fair.

It still sucked.

We'd both dreamed of the Olympics since we were little. We were so close. We'd spent two damn years here in Hackensack away from our friends and families, paying a fortune for scraps of our coach's attention. To not go to the Games after all this...

"What was it all for?" I muttered.

Head on my shoulder, Bree sniffed loudly. "Sometimes I don't know."

"Because we love skating?" I always had. I'd given up piano for it. But now I felt hollow.

Bree laughed humorlessly, sniffing again.

"Should that be a question?"

"Probably not? We do love it."

"We do. Most of the time. We don't have to love it all the time."

"Right." That was true. But I was afraid to tell her my love for skating was like a river that had slowed to a trickle.

She asked, "Did you see the text from Yaroslav?"

I was surprised he'd made the effort. His assistant, Svetlana, was the one who usually trained us. We were the bottom of the ladder, but we'd made the move hoping to break into the upper echelon. Sometimes, I honestly wasn't sure we had enough talent.

I said, "Not yet. I need to reply to my parents too."

Yaroslav was the hottest coach in ice dance at the moment, a former Russian champion who seemed to have cracked the code of producing winners and pleasing the judges. Training sites rose and fell, with all the top teams coming from Detroit for some years, then Montreal, and now Hackensack, New Jersey.

"He said, and I quote, 'This can defeat you or you can rise like phoenix.' So we'd better get feeling sorry for ourselves out of our systems before training in the morning."

I snorted. "I am definitely not expecting Yaroslav to be sympathetic." And I could admit that we were certainly feeling sorry for ourselves. We were allowed to wallow for a night. The thought of training in the morning had acid flooding my stomach. "Did you throw up?"

She exhaled hard, the air tickling my neck. "I tried not to."

"It's *not* your fault." This concussion was brutal. Some days she just couldn't keep food down.

"I should be better by now."

"It's not your fault." *I should have caught you.* "Did you eat tonight? I'll make soup."

"I'm not hungry."

"I'm making soup anyway."

"Okay."

I kept the light in the kitchen low as I warmed up the bone broth. I hated that this damn concussion made her so nauseous and dizzy. Some days she seemed so much better and then—*bam*—she could barely get out of bed.

I brought her the soup, but I was too anxious to eat yet myself. I cleaned the kitchen and paced the dark living room as she sipped slowly, the spoon scraping the bowl sometimes.

Finally, she said, "You're making me dizzy. Go run."

Even though I'd finished my cardio session at the gym before cleaning up everyone else's sweat, I laced up again and yanked on gloves and a hat. It was a gray, dank night, but there was no snow. Too warm for icy sidewalks, which was good.

Warm was an overstatement, but compared to Quebec? For sure. At home in Montreal, I'd be wearing more layers. There wasn't much wind as I started my usual loop of the suburb. The old houses were a little rundown like our apartment building, but it was fine.

Like a punch—*bam* in the face—I missed Vancouver. The foggy Pacific with driftwood on the beach. Mountains in the distance. Slowing my pace so Sam could keep up. Sam borrowing his parents' car so we could drive up to Whistler. Sam and me roaming Stanley Park. Sam's brown eyes lighting up as he laughed. Sam pretending to be bad at a new game to make me feel better about sucking.

Sam, Sam, Sam.

I'd been fourteen when I moved to Vancouver to train with Bree. Sure, Montreal would always be home in a way, but I didn't miss it like I missed Vancouver. Like I missed Sam.

When we'd moved to New Jersey to train with the winningest coaches in the world, I'd left my best friend because we needed to take it to the next level now or never. But was this all even worth it? Bree was hurt, and I missed Sam, and we worked so hard every day.

Taking another loop around a block of houses,

I ordered myself to stop thinking about Sam. Most people went away for university and didn't live in the same place as their best friends anymore. That was normal. I shouldn't miss him so much. I shouldn't think about him so much.

I shouldn't... Lots of things. There were lots of things I shouldn't do when it came to Sam.

I took the stairs back up, breathing a bit heavier as I reached the tenth floor. Bree still sat on the couch, the apartment totally dark again. As I took off my shoes, she asked, "Did you talk to Sam?"

"He's the one who told me the news. Chloe and Phillipe are there in Calgary. He missed the start of the men so he could tell me first."

Bree chuckled, and I asked, "What?" as I gulped a glass of water and flopped onto the other side of the couch.

"Our Olympic dream is probably over, but you can still get that look on your face."

I huffed. I knew—I wasn't that clueless—but still demanded, "What look?"

Her eyebrows shot up. "Oh, you're unaware? Let me explain."

Groaning, I shook my head. It was always a mistake not to ignore Bree's teasing. Always. At least she seemed to be feeling better after the broth.

"Whenever Sam comes up, you get the goofiest, softest expression. Your eyes go distant, like you're imagining his pretty face, and there's a tiny

22

smile on your lips. It's a Sam smile. I never see it for anyone else."

"That's not true," I muttered. "You can barely see me." We were in the dark, after all.

"I see you." She sat sideways and poked my thigh with her toe. "Also, I could be blindfolded and know you were making a Sam smile." She dropped the teasing voice. "Honestly, those are your only real smiles lately."

I shifted uncomfortably. "That's not true." Yeah, it had been tense and stressful this season after Bree's concussion. If I'd been quicker, it wouldn't have happened at all. I flashed her a performance smile. "See?" I said through my teeth.

She rolled her eyes. We sat in silence for a bit before she asked, "Are you ever going to tell him?"

I jerked, staring at her. "Tell him what?"

"Do you really want me to spell it out? I will, but—"

"No!" I held up a hand. I wasn't clueless about how I felt, but that didn't mean I spoke it out loud. "And are you kidding? No way. Never. Forget it."

"Wow. You're practically admitting it." She sounded genuinely shocked and leaned closer, squeezing my forearm. Even in the faint glow of streetlights, I could see how serious she was. "You're in love with him. Aren't you?"

Wait. No. How did we get here? After years of

teasing, we were actually talking about this for real? I must have been raw from the big news of the day. My usual defenses faltered. I never talked about it. Never.

But Bree was staring at me with so much love and compassion and like she was begging me to be honest with her. Her defenses had to be low too considering how sick she'd been for months now.

In that moment, after laughing it off for so long, I had to be honest with Bree. She deserved it. Holding my breath, I nodded.

She gripped my arm. "So tell him." When I shook my head, she asked, "Why not? It's like a cloud hanging over you."

"Because he's my best friend! My *straight* best friend." Tabarnak! This was bizarre to talk about out loud. When I woke up in the morning, I hadn't thought this day would end with Chloe and Phillipe returning to competition and me confessing my secret love for my best friend.

"I dunno about that."

My heart pounded like I was running again. "What? Sam's straight."

"Before we left Vancouver, I thought he was getting into you. Something about the way he looked at you changed."

"No way." My throat went dry. "Sam's not into me! He only hooks up with girls."

"In high school. But he's in university now. It's

been two years since we moved. How do you know for sure he hasn't been experimenting?"

The idea of Sam with other guys had me leaping to my feet and pacing on the cheap IKEA polka-dot rug. It had never occurred to me. I hated it. I hated it so much I thought I might puke or shout or run outside in my bare feet.

Bree whistled softly. "Guess you're the jealous type after all."

"I'm not jealous! And Sam's not fucking other guys! Or any guys. And he wouldn't want to fuck me."

"Okay. I'm sorry." Her face pinched. "Thank you for telling me, though. I mean, I always knew, but thank you."

I leaned down and kissed her cheek. "If I was ever going to tell anyone, of course it would be you." Sam was my best friend, but so was Bree. Just in a different way. "You always have my back."

"Always, babe. I just want you to be happy." She held up her hand and counted on her fingers. "You're happiest when you're playing piano, when Sam's around, and when we're scoring well. And when Sam's around." She tapped her baby finger. "Did I mention when Sam's around?"

I opened my mouth to argue, but could only come up with, "He's my best friend."

She sighed. "I know. You don't want to ruin a

good thing, right? Hey, you should see if he can come to Tremblant. If he'll be in Toronto for the holidays, maybe he can get away for a few days. It's not too far."

I'd been so busy with training and worrying about Bree's concussion that I hadn't even thought about it. My heart skipped. "Maybe?"

"Your family will be in Florida with your grandparents, and I'll be with Tim. I'm dying to see him. Have I mentioned that?"

I kept a straight face. "Who's Tim? Never heard of him."

"Oh, didn't I tell you I've been dating this guy since grade ten and that long distance sucks ass? He's flying out from Vancouver, and we're going to spend every second together that you and I aren't on the ice."

Her smile faded. "Assuming I can skate and my stupid head doesn't ruin everything. Because we need all the show money we can get if we're going to keep paying for ice time and coaching. But if Chloe and Phillipe are coming back, maybe it doesn't matter after all because we won't make the Olympics anyway. We might not even make Worlds again."

I swallowed hard. "Your head isn't stupid."

She winced as she stood, and I lunged forward to take her shoulders and keep her steady. She murmured, "Babe, I'm okay. No more dizziness—

just the headache."

Still, I walked her to bed and grabbed her a glass of water so she wouldn't have to get up in the night if she was thirsty. She smiled sadly and thanked me. Neither of us mentioned our Olympic dream again.

In her doorway, I whispered, "You really think Sam might be into me?"

"I really do. But I don't know for sure. I could ask him if you—"

"No! Nope. Do not ask him."

She smiled. "I promise I won't. Sleep tight."

Under a weak stream of hot water, I scrubbed clean before bed and tried to stop thinking about Sam. Especially Sam and other guys. Especially Sam being into *me* at the end of high school? Bree had to be wrong about that. There was no way.

If Sam wasn't straight, he'd have told me. We were best friends, and I was gay. His brother was gay. He helped organize the trans rights action group in high school. He definitely would have told me.

In my towel, dripping on the polka-dot rug, I paced again. My brain flipped between freaking out about Chloe and Phillipe taking our spot and the idea of Sam liking me back. Sam not being straight.

Obviously it was possible—he could be bi or pan or anything. Lots of people identified as straight growing up and then realized they weren't. Could Sam be hooking up with guys and not telling me for some reason?

I was wired with tension, and even when I got into bed and closed my eyes, my brain would not *shut up*. Olympics, Sam, Olympics, Sam, Bree's concussion, money, Sam, Olympics—was it worth all this sacrifice? Was Sam with other guys?

If so, why wasn't he with me?

I felt like I was coming out of a spin on the ice, and my brain decided to focus on the idea of Sam with me.

Naked.

My dick was really into the idea, and I latched onto it. Both my dick and the thought of Sam in my bed. I slept naked, and I fumbled for the lube in the drawer next to me. After getting myself nice and slick, I jerked while tweaking my nipples hard.

I'd had a million fantasies of Sam naked with me. I'd seen his bare body randomly—in the locker room after gym or changing when I slept over at the Sakaguchis' house. He'd filled out a bit since then, but it wasn't even his body I really fantasized about.

It was the way he laughed so hard sometimes that he snorted. It was that smile. The way it felt like the sun, warm on my face.

But I couldn't pretend I didn't also get off on imagining Sam kissing me. Touching me all over. I kicked off the covers and bent my legs, pressing my taint with slick fingers before pushing the middle finger into my hole.

Biting back a moan, I tilted my hips and crooked my finger to reach my gland. I gasped, careful to keep as quiet as possible since the walls were thin. Fuck, I loved fingering myself. I rode waves of bliss, working my cock with my other hand and breathing hard.

Sometimes, my mind went totally blank when I did this. But tonight, it was all Sam. Sam on top of me, my legs spread for him as he fucked me. Moaning in my ear, kissing me, sweaty and messy and *smiling*.

Straining, I pulled back my foreskin and thumbed the head of my leaking cock while I rubbed my prostate. Did Sam play with his ass? Would he like it? What would he think if he saw me now?

My back arched as I pretended Sam was watching me. Would he get off on this? Would he come inside me—would he come all over me?

Shaking, I spurted all over myself, imagining it was Sam's jizz painting my stomach and splashing my chest hair. Imagining he was smiling down at me, his new highlighted hair messy, his dimples huge.

On the mattress, my phone buzzed, and I just about jumped out of my cum-smeared skin as

Sam's face appeared on the screen, blinding in the darkness. I couldn't do a video chat like this, so I declined it but called him right back.

"Hey," I said. "Sorry, it's too dark for video." Not a lie, exactly.

"It's cool. You okay? You sound like you're working out."

I concentrated on slowing my breathing. "Just rushed to get the phone. How did Henry do?" I hadn't even looked up any of the results.

"Good! I barely made it back in time to see him. I didn't have my ticket, but one of the volunteers recognized me and convinced them Henry Sakaguchi's brother definitely wasn't trying to scam his way in. Anyway, he had a clean skate, but he's still in second. The judges are loving everything Theo does these days. He could probably pick his nose at center ice and win as long as he lands his jumps cleanly."

"Henry must hate him more than ever." Even though it was up to the judges, sometimes it was hard not to resent certain skaters for getting ridiculously high and undeserved performance scores.

Sam scoffed. "He'd like to think so, but Henry's too secretly soft to actually hate Theo. It's honestly adorable that he tries." After a pause, he asked, "How are you doing?"

"Fine." I yanked the covers over me, my face

hot even though Sam couldn't see me and had no way of knowing that I'd just jerked off.

Or that I'd been imagining him.

"Dude, come on."

"Yeah, okay. Not the greatest. I don't really want to talk about it. I don't know what to think. We've worked so hard for so many years, and now…"

"Yeah. It's not fair. I mean, it is, but it isn't."

"Exactly."

I didn't have to explain it to Sam. God, that was such an amazing feeling, and I missed him so much I was afraid I'd start crying. Calls and texts and playing League were all great, but I needed to see him. I needed my best friend.

"Can you come to Mont-Tremblant? I know you have to spend Christmas with your family, but just for a couple of days? It would be cool to hang in person."

He was silent, and I was about to tell him never mind when he said, "That would be *awesome*. I need to see my grandpa in Toronto for sure, but let me ask Mom and Dad. Henry won't care. But is there a place for me to stay? Not sure I have the money for a hotel room at Tremblant in December."

"You can stay with me! The performers all get little cabins. They're not paying us much, so it's one of the perks. Doubt there's a view, but…"

"Fuck the view. As long as we can hang, I'm in. I miss you, man."

My heart was ready to burst out of my chest. Now that Bree had put it in my head, I couldn't help but hope. Did Sam like me back? Was it possible?

No. I couldn't go down that path. I said, "This is going to be an amazing Christmas."

Sam was my best friend and nothing more. We'd get to hang in person again for the first time in way too long, and that was all. That was more than enough.

Chapter Three

Sam

HOLY CRAP. WHOEVER decked these fancy halls was *really* into Christmas and had a *huge* ladder.

Duffel bag tugging on my shoulder, I turned in a circle. The lobby of the Pinnacle Resort featured a massive ceiling with timber beams wrapped in glittering red garlands with green pine boughs that looked real. I couldn't be sure since they seemed a thousand feet up.

The place was not only huge but extremely shiny and plush. Everything looked brand new, which I guess it was since the resort had only opened in the summer. It was all glass, wood, and velvet, but in a modern way. Aside from the employees behind the long reception desk, there were only a few people around.

The front of the marble-floored lobby was a huge window showing an amazing view of Mont-Tremblant's village below, the lights bright and festive as evening set in. The Christmas tree in the corner was so big that, seriously, did they get a fire truck to swing by and extend its ladder?

The tree was decorated in gold and silver, and the star on top shone. An instrumental carol played softly, and the air smelled of cinnamon and fresh pine. I enjoyed the holidays as much as the next person—presents, delicious food, and time off were all awesome—but this was, like, *professional* Christmas commitment. This was next level.

"*Joyeux Noël!* Merry Christmas!"

I turned to find a young woman in a navy hotel uniform holding out a small tray of full-sized candy canes and foil-wrapped chocolates. At least I assumed they were chocolates since they were in the shape of truffles. With a gleaming smile, she extended the tray.

Her dark hair was twisted on her head, and I swear there was a faint dusting of gold on her brown skin—but maybe that was the reflection from the decorations. Or expensive blush from Sephora.

I stuffed my gloves in my coat pockets. "Thanks! Merry Christmas." My stomach growled, but I limited myself to one candy cane and two chocolates, which was probably still too many.

She didn't seem judgy. "Did you just arrive?"

"Yeah. I took the bus up from Toronto. My family and I opened our presents and stuff last night on Christmas Eve."

Not that she cared. Why was I babbling? I was weirdly nervous. I guess I felt out of place in this hotel that I couldn't afford? I realized I'd never really traveled without my family.

"How lovely. Are you a skier?"

I motioned to my puffy yellow and black-trimmed North Face jacket. "No, it's just for show. And to stay warm. I've tried snowboarding in Whistler a few times, but I suck."

She chuckled, all white teeth and smooth tone. "If you're interested in lessons, we'd be happy to arrange it."

"Oh, I can't afford that. I'm not even really staying here." Suddenly I felt like she'd call security on my ass. Why was I so jumpy?

But her smile didn't waver. "Are you visiting a guest?"

"Yeah, my best friend." Excitement skittered through me. "He's a figure skater in your holiday show. He's performing tonight, so I guess I'll chill in his room."

"Ah, one of our visiting artists. I believe the skaters are housed in our staff accommodation in Spruce Grove. If you care to wait a moment, I'll check that you're in the system. What's your friend's name? And yours? I'm Alice."

"Sam Sakaguchi. My friend is Etienne Allard. Thanks for your help."

I loitered near the tree. It was just past seven p.m. on Christmas Day, and most guests were probably at dinner.

In fact, the restaurant had to be close since I could smell roast meat that made my mouth water. I'd grabbed a mediocre egg salad sandwich for lunch when the bus stopped on the way to Montreal, and I was so ready for real food.

Alice returned. "Your name hasn't been added in the system, so I'm afraid I can't give you a key to the cabin."

I groaned inwardly. Along with real food, I was very ready for a hot shower to wash off the bus grime. It had taken almost ten hours to get here. "Can I store my bag? I'm going to walk down to the village and grab dinner."

"Of course. Unless you want to see the show? It starts shortly and there might be an empty seat left." She arched a very plucked brow, her silky voice dropping into a more real tone. "If you're into figure skating, that is."

See Etienne now? Hell yeah. Food could wait. "I am, actually. That would be awesome." My stomach swooped with that weird nervousness again. I was finally going to see Etienne in person again. It'd been more than a year since I'd last seen him at a competition Henry skated in too.

But that was dumb. I'd seen him a million times on my phone. Just that morning when he called to say merry Christmas with bedhead and stubble. There was no reason to be *nervous* either way.

I was squeezing the truffles, which I realized too late, the chocolate going soft in my sweaty palm. I'd have to lick it off the wrapper at this point. Tempting, but I tossed them in the discreet garbage can and pocketed the plastic-wrapped candy cane for later.

Alice stowed my duffel in the luggage room before leading me along a corridor off the lobby. She explained how the resort had a full-sized indoor rink as well as an outdoor skating trail winding through a flat area of the forest.

I nodded and tried to pay attention as we passed conference rooms, my pulse up and stomach flipping. I was hungry, which was why I was being so weird. But I was allowed to be excited to finally see Etienne. Of course I was.

Because technology was great, but it wasn't the same as seeing your best friend in person. Hugging him. Smelling his cologne—a fresh, ocean/rosemary scent that Bree bought for him every Christmas because she loved the smell. They joked that even once they retired, she'd still send him a bottle or else he'd go back to the drug store

Adidas scent he used to wear.

The one she gave him was Armani. Not super expensive but still nice. When my mom made rosemary mashed potatoes last year at Thanksgiving, I kept thinking about hugging Etienne.

"Sam?"

I realized Alice had stopped and was staring at me. I said, "Uh-huh?"

"This way." She motioned to a long, glass-enclosed walkway strung with golden fairy lights, red bows and holly dangling from timber beams overhead. It was a little cooler in the walkway, but it was still heated.

"Wow," I said as we continued. The floor by the conference room had been carpeted, but this glass connection to the arena was the same marble as the lobby. My Timberland boots squeaked. "Mopping must be someone's full-time job."

She smirked. "Yep."

I could see lit cabins in the distance behind the hotel complex, and Alice explained that the resort had a hotel in the main building with the lobby as well as self-contained cabins in different sections on the property.

Inside the arena, Alice talked to a guy in a suit, and before long I was seated in the back row. There were only ten rows of seats and no boards around the ice, so it felt quite small. Not in a bad way, though. It was... What was the right word?

Intimate.

The seats were padded and actually comfortable, which was a minor miracle. I unzipped my puffy jacket, giving the old woman beside me an apologetic smile as I fidgeted. Most people must have come through the glass walkway since they weren't wearing coats. The seats were comfy, but there still wasn't a lot of elbow room. I was on the aisle at least, and a free ticket to see Etienne was an awesome Christmas present.

The lights dimmed, and the opening bells of "All I Want for Christmas is You" chimed. As the song kicked into gear, a skater wearing tight red pants and a painted-on green tee burst out of the curtained access tunnel with a wide grin. I blinked in surprise to see Theo Sullivan, my brother's nemesis. I didn't think this show had any big headliners.

Not that Etienne and Bree weren't awesome, but they weren't at the Stars on Ice tour level like Henry and Theo. Theo reeled off a triple Lutz-triple toe combo like it was nothing. Which I guess it was since he normally did quads.

His jumps were amazing—not that I'd ever say that in Henry's earshot—and it was fun watching him play to the audience. Theo didn't have the deep edges and flow that Henry did, but he could put on a show.

After Theo's solo, the rest of the skaters took

the ice for a group number to "Jingle Bell Rock." There was Etienne, gliding out holding Bree's hand. The male skaters all wore the same outfit as Theo while the women were in white-trimmed Santa dresses. I cheered for Etienne and Bree as they were announced, putting my fingers in my mouth and whistling.

The lady beside me gave me a strange look, but whatever. I was making sure my best friend got the applause he deserved. I watched Etienne and Bree in the corner of the rink performing their rotational helicopter lift, Bree sitting on his shoulder with her long legs extended forward and back as he spun.

The skaters met at one end of the ice, skating together down the rink in a choreographed sequence. Etienne was smiling and didn't miss a step, but I could see that he was tense and thinking through it. They'd only learned the routine a few days ago.

I didn't know how Etienne could breathe in that costume, let alone skate and shake his ass. The red pants did make his ass look great, though. Not that I was really looking or anything. I was used to him looking like a model in anything he wore.

The performance was seventy-five minutes with no intermission, which was perfect. It was a fun holiday show, and Etienne and Bree's solo number to "Hallelujah" seemed to go over well with the crowd. It had been their exhibition routine last season and fit in well enough with the Christmas theme. All the skaters had their own routines to bring to a show so whoever was choreographing just had to do the group numbers and maybe a couple of others.

I noticed they'd modified one of their spins so that Bree was upright instead of bent with her head low by her foot. I hoped she wasn't feeling dizzy again. Etienne had said she was doing better this week, but it was so up and down.

Fat snowflakes drifted from the sky outside, and I tried to catch one on my tongue as I waited alone in the still night. I guess I could have waited inside, but after all day on buses, I wanted the fresh air. The arena was also strung with gold lights and was clad in wood unlike the typical concrete suburban hockey arena. Everything at Pinnacle looked upscale.

"Sam, right?"

I retracted my tongue and found Theo watching me with an easy grin, his cheeks dimpled. The snow caught in his damp, light brown hair. "Merry Christmas! Is Henry here too?"

"No, he's in Toronto. And yeah, I'm Sam." I extended my hand, and we shook. "Merry Christmas. Great show!" Our breath clouded in the crisp air as we spoke.

"Thanks. I hope Henry's taking a break from

training over the holidays?"

"Nope."

Theo frowned. "He's going to burn out if he's not careful. Or injure himself."

What did Theo care? "That would work out pretty well for you."

He seemed to shake off any concern. "Nah. I'd rather keep on beating him fair and square. No offense."

I had to laugh. "None taken. I know Henry can beat you next season at the Olympics when it counts."

Theo flashed his dimples. "Guess we'll find out."

"I was surprised to see you here. Aren't you afraid you'll burn *yourself* out performing twice a day for two weeks? It's a tough schedule."

"Are you kidding? Performing is the best part of skating. If I could do this and not spend all my life in the practice rink, I'd be set." He shrugged. "But you don't get to headline shows unless you win big competitions."

"Fair. There wasn't anything closer to home?"

Theo shuddered. "Being as far from home as possible was the whole point. Besides, it's gorgeous here."

I remembered belatedly that his mom was a notoriously overbearing skating mother. Luckily for Henry, our parents were chill. They let him do his thing and cheered him on—and had spent a lot on his skating over the years—but they just wanted him to be happy. With a pang, I missed not being with them on Christmas even though we'd done a big dinner the night before.

I made small talk with Theo, which felt a little disloyal to Henry, but I wasn't going to freeze out the guy. It was Christmas, and he seemed a little lonely. I almost asked him if he wanted to have a late dinner with us or something, but he left before I could.

Then Etienne appeared, and he grabbed me in a huge hug, almost lifting me off my feet. Laughing, I slapped his back, and amid the fresh smell of the falling snow, I inhaled that faint, familiar rosemary and ocean cologne along with his unique scent. His neck was still damp from his post-performance shower. He squeezed me tightly, the hug going on.

And on. He slapped my back this time. "Merry Christmas, man."

"Merry Christmas!" Bree exclaimed. She held out her arms, her hair tucked under a purple toque.

I had to let go of Etienne to hug her. It was probably getting weird at that point anyway—we were bros, not long-lost lovers like the ones on that time-travel show Obaachan watched. I hugged Bree and her boyfriend, Tim. He was very tall and quiet, and he adored her. As he should.

I went to grab my bag from reception and said thanks again to Alice. Soon enough, Etienne and I were alone. We followed a plowed walking path through the trees, big snowbanks on either side.

"Wow, there's so much snow here. Toronto had a green Christmas."

Etienne grimaced. "It's not Christmas without a ton of snow. I always hated that in Vancouver. Hey, how's your grandfather doing?"

"Not bad! Still won't wear his hearing aids, but he seems happy in the old folks' home. We brought him over to the rental house for dinner. They all say Merry Christmas, by the way."

"Same from my family. They went to the beach and are having a barbecue."

"Cool." I wanted to ask what they thought about Chloe and Phillipe coming out of retirement, but I wasn't about to bring that up on Christmas. Etienne hadn't been up for talking about it the last couple of weeks. I guessed he was processing, and I didn't want to push.

The path was lit with strings of golden fairy lights wound around wooden railings. I supposed it was like a boardwalk in summer. We passed big cabins with lots of space between them and covered porches. I squinted. "Is that a hot tub?"

"Yeah. All the cabins in Le Bois-du-Nord have them, and the really deluxe ones up on Eagle

Ridge and the Skyline."

"And Spruce Grove?" I asked hopefully.

He cut me a dubious look. "Dream on. Though there's a communal sauna for each block of cabins. Could be worse."

Etienne led me off the main path, snow crunching under our boots as we veered deeper into the forest. There were no Christmas lights decorating the staff area, but with the moon reflecting on the snow, we didn't need them.

"Wow," I said quietly. "It's so peaceful." Aside from our footsteps, the snow-capped forest seemed silent.

"No music or partying allowed. A lot of the hotel staff live in the village, but I guess the cabins are good for out-of-towners."

These cabins were spaced much more closely together than the guest variety, and there were no porches or hot tubs. Light only shone from a few. Etienne punched in a code on the door of one, and I followed him inside.

He flicked on the lights, and I was surprised to see sparkly garlands strung up around the square room. The little kitchenette to the right had a microwave and mini-fridge with a big red bow on the front.

Etienne bent to pull off his mukluk-style boots before crossing to the bed and plugging in the multi-colored lights wound around the rustic bedposts and across the top of the spindled headboard. The cabin's one window over the bed had snowflakes sprayed on the glass with that fake snow in a can and a stencil.

I laughed. "Festive!"

"Bree's work. You should see her cabin." He whistled softly. "I think she bought out the Christmas store in the village."

I was taking off my boots and coat when I realized the lit bed was also the *only* bed. For some reason, I'd been thinking of a standard hotel room with two beds in it. But the cabin was what the resort probably called "cozy" or "snug." A.k.a. real small.

Etienne hadn't made the bed, and the red and black plaid duvet was in a pile at the foot of the mattress. The plaid matched the curtains on the window. The mattress was a double at most. A full, I think they called them? Definitely not a queen. Which was fine!

"Okay?" Etienne asked.

I croaked, "Uh-huh! Thirsty."

He hung his coat on a hook beside the door and poured me a glass of water from the tap. "Sorry there's only one bed. I could ask them if there's a rollaway I can sleep on? They probably don't charge too much for it." He handed me the glass, our fingers brushing.

Shaking my head, I gulped the tepid water.

"Nah. It's fine. Remember that time on the school trip to Tofino when we had to share that tiny tent? This is luxury."

He laughed. "Yeah. You almost gave me a black eye with your elbow in the middle of the night."

"I'll try not to mess up your good looks this time."

"Better not! The Pinnacle's paying me the big bucks for this." He motioned to his face, giving one of his fake skater smiles. He dropped the smile just as quickly, flopping onto the end of the bed. "Did you eat? I'm starving."

"Me too. I mean, no, I didn't eat."

"Pizza? They'll deliver it to the side of the hotel. Takes too long to bring it all the way back here. I'll get it." He was already tapping his phone. "They're fast."

"Perfect. Can I grab a shower? I'm surprised you were willing to hug me with this bus stink all over me."

"Is that what that was?" He wrinkled his nose. "I wasn't going to say anything, but…"

I picked up a plaid throw cushion from the chair by the wooden dresser against the front wall of the cabin and threw it at him. "Shut up."

The bathroom was to the left of the festive bed. It was a decent size and tiled in simple white. I eagerly stripped off and stayed under the powerful stream of hot water long enough that the mirror steamed over completely.

With one of the white towels slung around my waist, I opened the door and poked my head out of the bathroom to get a gulp of cool air. Etienne was gone, presumably off to meet the pizza guy. My stomach growled at the thought, and I padded barefoot to the kitchen to poke around.

Aside from Etienne's gross protein powder, a carton of eggs, and various vegetables, there wasn't much. I remembered the candy cane and fished it out of my coat pocket. Still damp, I sat on the end of the bed and peeled the crinkly wrapper.

Mmm. Sugar.

It was Christmas Day. I wasn't eating vegetables unless they were roasted in butter. Well, I'd make an exception for the pineapple and mushrooms on the pizza. Though pineapples weren't a vegetable. No, they had to be a fruit.

I shivered in the *whoosh* of cold air as Etienne returned. Candy cane in my mouth, I blinked up at him in the doorway. Goosebumps rippled over my skin, my nipples going hard. Pulling out the candy cane, I frowned.

"Dude, it's freezing! Close the door!"

Etienne jolted and slammed it shut, leaning back against the heavy wood. He was still staring at me, gripping the pizza box.

"Hey, pineapple's a fruit, right? Not a vegetable?" I licked across the rounded top of the candy cane.

"What?" he rasped.

"You know how tomatoes are actually fruit? Are there fruits that are really vegetables?"

He thrust out the pizza box. "Take this?"

"Oh, sure."

I sucked the candy cane back into my mouth so both my hands were free. As I stood, the towel slipped. I caught it and re-tucked it around my hips before taking the box. Etienne bent to take off his boots. He fiddled with them a long time, adjusting them on a mat by the door. When he stood, his face was beet red.

"Pineapples are fruit." He took back the pizza, turning to the kitchenette. "Want to watch something?"

"Sure." I turned on the TV sitting on top of the dresser across from the foot of the bed and grabbed my boxer shorts and sleeping T-shirt from my bag. I hung the towel in the bathroom, squishing it to the left side of the bar so Etienne would know which one was mine.

The cabin smelled like cheese and grease and meat, and I groaned appreciatively as I got settled on the bed. "Ho-ho hell yes."

Etienne laughed weakly and passed me a plate with three slices crammed on it as well as a garlic dipping sauce he'd known to order for me without asking.

It was also our usual pizza order—regular crust, extra sauce, extra cheese, sausage, ham, pineapple, and mushrooms. We'd agreed on these toppings years ago and never deviated. It was weirdly comforting.

As I flipped channels, my mouth full of delicious pizza, Etienne changed into his PJs. When he was a kid, his family had done the matching holiday pajamas, but he was only wearing normal flannel bottoms and a ratty Skate Canada tee.

It was so worn around the collar that it was stretched out of shape and dipped below his left collarbone. The wiry ends of his chest hair brushed the dip below the bone.

"Don't you sleep naked anymore?" I asked for some weird reason.

Etienne stared. "Um, yeah. When I'm by myself or…"

"Right, right." The bed squeaked as I fidgeted.

"You want to watch the Mormon Tabernacle Choir?"

"Huh?" I turned my gaze from his old tee back to the TV. "Oh, sorry." I kept flipping, and we both exclaimed, "Yes!" when I hit pay dirt.

John McClane was tapping the ancient screen in the lobby of Nakatomi Plaza and being butthurt that Holly was using her own name.

"It just started too!" Etienne grinned around a

mouthful of pizza.

"It's a Christmas miracle." He'd gotten me a can of beer from the fridge, and I popped the top and held it up for a cheers.

We devoured the pizza and called out iconic lines along with the actors.

Etienne put on a fake serious face as we said in unison, "You throw quite a party. I didn't realize they celebrated Christmas in Japan."

This was one of our faves since when I was a kid, someone had actually asked me why my family celebrated Christmas—as if my parents weren't born in Canada, where pretty much everyone did Christmas in my experience. Hashtag not-all-Canadians, but mostly everyone I knew.

We groaned at Takagi's cringey answering line about Pearl Harbor, which I couldn't see making it into a movie these days. Eighties movies had a huge cringe factor. *Die Hard* got a pass on being the best Christmas movie ever, and no, it wasn't up for debate as to whether it was really a Christmas movie. It was. The end.

And being here in this cozy cabin with my best friend, eating pizza on the bed and watching a holiday classic, was an awesome Christmas. Shit, I really had missed Etienne so much. I almost reached over and hugged him and told him that.

But it would be weird, right? Instead, I took another gulp of beer and shouted out the next line.

Chapter Four

Etienne

I'D IMAGINED THIS moment so many times, but I'd never pictured waking up with Sam under the glow of Christmas lights in a cabin in the mountains. The colors were like a rainbow over his slack face. His lips looked particularly pink and tempting.

He was sprawled on his stomach, his right knee sticking out. Curled on my side facing him, I'd only have to shift an inch and our knees would touch. I'd only have to shift a bit farther to kiss those pink lips.

Obviously, I wouldn't.

His green-tipped hair stuck up wildly in the glow of the colored lights. He hugged the pillow to his face and neck. The plaid duvet had slipped down to the middle of his back, and I worried he was cold, but I didn't want to wake him by adjusting it.

The memory of Sam's nipples peaking in the cold air invaded. When I'd opened the door and found him there, damp-skinned and only in the towel, that candy cane in his mouth…

Tabarnak.

No more thinking of Sam practically naked and sucking things. Not when I was in bed with him, my morning wood threatening to grow into a giant sequoia like the ones on Vancouver Island. It was ridiculous—we'd slept in the same bed before in high school. Or in the same tent, like on that trip to Tofino.

It felt different now. I couldn't understand why. This was the longest we'd gone since we met in grade nine without seeing each other in person. But we still talked and texted and played League of Legends every week. We were still best friends. Nothing should be different. Nothing should have changed.

"Before we left Vancouver, I thought he was getting into you."

Was Bree right? I'd tried not to think about it. Between rehearsal for the show and the news about Chloe and Phillipe, I'd had my fill of worry. Not to mention Bree's concussion. She'd insisted on not saying anything to the people in charge. So far, she'd been okay. No really bad days, and yesterday had been really good.

We'd modified our exhibition number to avoid the moves that seemed to affect her the most. We hadn't discussed the Olympics again aside from agreeing that we'd get through these holiday performances first. Nationals were at the end of January. In the new year, we could talk about the future.

For the next week and a half, I had to worry about two shows a day, and that was enough. That and how I'd sleep inches away from Sam without kissing him. He was staying through New Year's, and it would be awesome.

I had to piss, but I didn't want to get up and wake him. Sam had trouble sleeping sometimes. He could fall asleep okay but woke up easily. He looked so peaceful. Pissing could wait.

And obviously I wasn't going to kiss him because it would ruin everything. Sam wasn't into me. He'd never even hinted at being anything but straight. He'd have said something.

Unless he hadn't known?

That surge of hope in my stupid heart was only going to make this worse. I'd been putting off dating anyone seriously for too long. I'd hooked up when I needed to, and training kept me busy and exhausted. But how much longer was I going to dream?

Sam snorted and mumbled as he stirred. I shut

my eyes, going rigid. I didn't want him to think I was being a creeper watching him while he slept. He'd never been freaked out that I was gay. I'd told him when we were sixteen, and he'd said, "*Cool.*"

That was it, just that one word. I knew his brother was gay and his family was totally supportive, but I'd still been nervous. Probably because I was afraid he'd know I was in love with him. But he still hadn't figured it out. Or had he? And maybe my feelings weren't as one-sided as I thought? Maybe?

I flipped to my other side, cursing Bree for putting the idea in my head. It was wishful thinking.

Sam yawned and mumbled, "'Morning. Is it morning?"

After stretching and pretending I'd just woken, I sat up to peek between the drawn curtains. "Yep. Sunny. It's after nine." I hadn't slept this late in forever.

Rolling over, Sam stretched, making a cute little noise as his back arched. His tee had bunched up, and I stared at the soft, exposed skin. His belly was smooth, but there were a few hairs poking up from the waistband of his boxers.

I catapulted out of bed and escaped into the bathroom to finally piss, but I had to breathe calmly for a minute before I could. Jesus, I was acting like I was fourteen again and having all these new, exciting, confusing feelings for Sam. I should have been over this crush years ago.

It wasn't a crush, which was the entire problem.

My lucky robe hung on a hook, so at least I didn't have to go back out in a towel. I shut down the memory of Sam sucking that candy cane, the towel slipping down his hips...

The white terrycloth robe was faded and dingy. I should probably bleach it, but I was afraid it would disintegrate. I didn't even put it in the dryer anymore. I'd swiped it from the hotel in China after Bree and I won our first junior international competition. The robe came everywhere with me.

Sam was stretched out on the bed, scrolling his phone in one hand and idly scratching his belly with the other. I said, "Bathroom's free!" too energetically.

He only said, "Cool," so maybe he didn't notice I was being strange. Or maybe he was used to it. He shuffled into the bathroom, yawning again, still scrolling.

As I tugged on my gray, stretchy practice clothes, I cursed myself again for being so wound up. I had to forget what Bree had said. She had to be wrong. There was just no way Sam was into me. The shower ran in the bathroom, and I tried my best not to think of him wet and soapy.

I normally turned on the coffee machine first thing, so I did it now, fidgeting as I waited for it to heat. The hotel was big on being environmentally friendly, so it was a machine without the pods, but the coffee was way better.

Behind me, the bathroom door opened, and Sam moaned. "Mmm. That smells amazing."

When I turned, of course he was only wearing the towel around his waist. It wasn't that he was all buff with a six-pack or whatever. He was slim and what people would probably call "average." But he was *Sam*. Screw six-packs. I wanted to rub my face all over his soft belly and lick his nipples and smell his hairy armpits.

The machine poured a stream into the mug, and I added two packs of sugar and two fiddly little containers of cream before facing Sam again. "Double—"

Towel pooled at his feet, Sam bent over his duffle, ass just...right there. He stepped into his black boxer briefs and pulled them up, glancing over his shoulder.

"Double," I finished.

"Thanks, man. You didn't have to give me the first cup." He took it from me with a smile.

"No prob!" I jabbed at the machine and put another mug under the spout. I had to limit sugar, and I'd been drinking my coffee black for a few years. I burned my tongue gulping it too fast.

"I almost forgot—merry Christmas. Belated-ly." Sam held out a little clumsily wrapped package. It was mostly tape and a piece of snowman paper bent around a narrow object.

"What?" I took it hesitantly. "We never give each other presents."

"I know." He shrugged and sipped his coffee. "It's nothing. Made me think of you, that's all."

Pulse racing, I pried off the tape and ripped the paper open to find a black Batman key chain, the wings spread wide. There was a half-circle hole under the pointy-eared head. It took me a second. "Oh! A bottle opener?"

"Yep." He grinned. "Remember when we brought in the contraband beer to the movies and realized the stupid bottles weren't twist-tops?"

I laughed. "How could I forget? Trying to slam them open on the arm rests without breaking the bottles as the beer got warm as piss and all shaken. Why the hell didn't we bring cans?"

"Because we were dumbasses. And it was that Batman movie we went to see. So, next time you need a bottle opener…"

"Hopefully I won't be in a movie theater." I dug around in my suitcase for my keys and attached the new ring. "Thank you. I don't have anything for you, though."

He scoffed. "Hello, I'm crashing in your cabin and getting a vacation. And the key chain was, like, ten bucks."

"Thanks."

As we drank our coffee and relaxed against propped-up pillows, scrolling our phones, Sam's words echoed in my head like the sweetest music.

"Made me think of you."

I told myself to cut the shit and opened Instagram. Naturally, the first pic in my feed was Chloe Desjardins and Phillipe Vincent's Christmas post from yesterday. They were sitting in front of a roaring fire with their rescue dogs, both of them managing to look glamorous in matching reindeer flannel pajamas.

Ugh.

"What?" Sam asked beside me.

I must've made a disgusted noise out loud. "Nothing. Just Chloe and Phillipe being perfect and grateful and loving everyone on Insta." I flashed the screen at him.

He grimaced. "I wish they weren't so nice."

"*I know.* But they are. I didn't realize how much until we moved to Hackensack. We're not even competition for the top teams, but no one's nice. Yaroslav says you can be friendly, or you can be a champion."

"That's bullshit," Sam said firmly. "Henry's been world champion, and he's more than nice. He's one of the kindest people I've ever met. And…" He hesitated. "I know it's good to train in a competitive environment. It breeds champions and all that. But when you and Bree were coached by Laura back home, people were nice, weren't they?"

"Yeah. It was so different there." I breathed through a pang of longing. "But Yaroslav coaches six of the top teams in the world. Can't argue with success." I stared at the picture of Chloe and Phillipe. "At least they'll be back with their coaches in Montreal."

"You should unfollow them. Forget about what they're doing and focus on your own training."

"I wish, but if I unfollowed them, fans would notice. We can't look like we're salty about them coming back."

"Well…" He sighed. "Yeah. I wish I could say no one would notice your unfollows, but I've seen enough of the diehard skating fans to know better."

We lapsed into silence again, sipping and scrolling. Even though we hadn't seen each other in person for more than a year, we could have been back in high school. It was still so comfortable between us, which was a relief. I didn't know what I'd do without this. And if it could be more…

Nope, forget it, don't go down that path.

A text from Bree appeared at the top of my screen, and my gut clenched.

Hey. Feeling a little dizzy. Can we push back practice half an hour?

"What?" Sam asked. I hadn't realized I'd made any sound and glanced at him. He added, "You did that little worried sigh thing instead of your annoyed/stressed sigh. Though this sigh is also stressed."

I had to smile before I said, "Bree's 'a little dizzy,' which means a lot."

"Shit. What happens if she can't perform this afternoon? Or tonight?"

"I don't know. It's never happened before." The knot in my stomach tied itself into loop after loop. "If I'd caught her—"

"You did! You broke her fall."

"She still hit her head."

Sam sat up straighter. "Dude. You two were standing on the ice talking to your coach and she dropped like a stone. It was your quick reflexes that saved her from cracking her skull open. It's not your fault."

I shuddered to remember the movement from the corner of my eye as she went down. I'd lunged and then we were both on the ice. She'd hung limp in my arms, so pale I was afraid she was dead.

"It's. Not. Your. Fault," Sam repeated, poking me in the side with each word.

"She was dehydrated. I should have told Yaroslav she needed another day off after that flu."

"Right, but she insisted she was fine, and neither of you wanted to look weak."

"It wasn't as if Yaroslav would have even paid attention to us that day. But if anyone has to skip training, *then* he'll sure as hell pay attention."

"He sucks. Have you guys ever thought… I dunno. That maybe it's not worth it to train there?"

My heart skipped, bile rising in my throat. What was it all for if we didn't get to the Olympics? *Was* it worth it? I squashed the fear down. "We can't just leave. You don't walk away from the best coach and the top training center."

I jumped to my feet, anxious energy taking control. I said, "Anyway, it's the holidays. You're on vacation. You don't need to worry about this stuff."

Sam frowned. "It's not a problem or whatever. We can talk about this."

"I know! It's cool." There was already such a massive thing I couldn't talk to Sam about, and fear tugged at me. It was all snowballing. I needed to get in control of my feelings. My life. But not now. Later. "You hungry? Let's eat."

I tapped out a quick reply to Bree, telling her to take as long as she needed. It was ten, and the matinee was at three, so hopefully she'd be feeling steady by then.

The hotel restaurant was way out of my budg-

et, so we walked down into the village. It teemed
with people. The little shops had Boxing Day sale
signs in the windows in French and English, and
sun glinted off fresh snow on the ski hills rising up.
I pushed the worry and fear away. I was with Sam
in this awesome place, and we could enjoy the next
couple of hours.

"Hey, Sam!"

We turned at the door of a cafe, and a beautiful girl approached, smiling brightly. My heart
sank. She was the woman from reception Sam had
gone out of his way to be nice to last night. It
shouldn't bother me. Of course he should be nice
to her! I should be too. She got him in to see me
skate.

Jealousy still knifed me in the gut.

"Hi, Alice." Sam smiled. "You remember
Etienne?"

"Of course." She turned her friendly grin to
me. "Your skater BFF." She wore sleek snowpants
and a matching jacket in deep purple that looked
great with her brown skin and metallic lipstick.
Her black toque had ear flaps and she should have
been on a tourism poster.

I tried to smile back. "Hello." We were block-
ing the door and shuffled a few steps over on the
little pedestrian street. A huge bough of mistletoe
under a massive bow was attached to the lamppost
behind us. It mocked me.

To Sam, Alice said, "What are you up to while your pal works?"

He shrugged. "Just chilling."

"If you want to come snowboarding with us, we have an extra pass." She gestured over her shoulder toward a small group who were hanging back waiting for her. "My friend works at the ski resort and can sneak us in past the rental lines and hook us up with boards. The lift lines will still be brutal, but it'll be way faster."

"Oh, thanks! That sounds cool. I don't have ski pants, though," Sam said. "And I would fall a *lot*."

She laughed. "You can rent the pants too. And same, trust me."

"Cool. Maybe? We were just getting breakfast though, and you look ready."

"Grab it to go!" She reached out and touched his arm. "It'll be fun, I promise."

Sam had dated girls before. There was no reason for me to want Alice to go snowboard off a cliff. I couldn't remember ever feeling this stupidly jealous, and it was not a good look. So I said, "You should go! I ate too much last night anyway. Coffee will do before the matinee. Besides, I need to check on Bree." I backed away from Sam, who blinked at me in confusion.

"But you should eat something." He motioned to the cafe. "We still have time before you have to work."

"Nah, I'm good. Go! Have fun!"

"But…" Sam opened and closed his mouth. "Okay, cool."

Alice grinned. "Yay! This place has delish breakfast sandwiches. I'll wait out here. Too hot inside now that I'm geared up."

Sam nodded and asked me, "You sure you don't want anything?"

"Yep. Not hungry. I'll head back and check on Bree. Have fun today!" I held out my fist for a bro-y bump. Sam was on vacation. He should definitely go snowboarding with a gorgeous girl. I couldn't be selfish.

Sam bumped my fist and disappeared inside the cafe. The door was barely closed when Alice asked, "So what's his deal? Girlfriend? Boyfriend?"

"Neither."

"He's into girls?"

"Uh-huh." I stepped back, but Alice followed.

"What's his type?"

"Um, nothing specific. You're gorgeous, so I'm sure you're everyone's type."

She beamed and lightly slapped my arm. "Stop." Her smile vanished, her expression coy. "But don't."

I had to laugh. "Sense of humor is a big factor. So yeah, you're good."

Alice smiled. "Cool, thanks. He's a cutie. I

could use a holiday fling."

"So could he." It was true. Mandy dumped him months ago, and Sam was too sweet and funny and generous and hot to be single for too long. I backed up again. "I'll leave you to it."

"Thanks, Etienne. Happy skating? I'm not sure if 'break a leg' is appropriate." She frowned. "Is the Bree you mentioned your partner? Is she okay?"

"Yeah, she's good." I backed into an older woman and quickly apologized. Turning to Alice, I waved. "Not a problem. Thanks for asking. Have fun!"

I practically ran up to the Pinnacle. After texting Tim, who told me Bree was napping, I changed and hit the hotel gym. It was off-limits to most staff, but I had special access as a "visiting artist."

Pumping up the volume on my workout mix, I raced my best time on the treadmill before crunching and planking and squatting and lunging. Trying to think of anything but Sam tumbling into a snowbank with Alice like a scene out of a rom-com.

Bree texted that she felt better and would meet me at the arena to warm up and run through the group numbers with the cast, so I headed there still sweaty and jittery from another coffee. I'd eat after the matinee show.

In the backstage area, I'd just laced my skates

when I checked my phone and saw the wall of texts from Tim. My heart skipped glancing though his worried messages, and Bree walked in, putting on a smile.

"Morning!" she said with a fake cheeriness that could not mask that her skin was practically gray under the makeup she normally wouldn't have applied until closer to showtime.

"No," I said. "Forget it. I'm taking you back to your cabin."

One of the skaters in an armchair looked up from her phone and said, "Oh, shit! What happened?"

As Bree lied about nothing being wrong, I quickly tapped out a reply to Tim saying I was on it. Bree stiffly bent her knees, keeping her head upright as she sat on the edge of a chair. This was clearly one of the days when bending over made her horribly dizzy. She'd probably puked multiple times.

"No," I said again, coming over to sit beside her.

Bree's mouth tightened. "I'm. Fine," she gritted out.

Theo Sullivan walked in eating a banana. Mouth full, his eyes widened, and he mumbled, "Whoa! What happened?"

Bree's eyes filled with tears she blinked away,

refusing to let them fall. I rubbed her back gently. "It's not your fault. You can't go on today."

"I have to. We have a job to do."

The director, Matthieu, walked in right on cue, other skaters trickling in behind him. The chatter ceased, everyone's attention zeroing in on Bree. Matthieu, a man in his fifties with a shaved head who wore black turtlenecks and red-framed glasses, stopped short.

He exhaled sharply. "Injury?"

As Bree said no, I said, "Yes. She had a concussion months ago. Having a bad day." We should have disclosed that she still had symptoms before taking the job. We knew this. But we'd hoped it would all turn out fine.

"*Sacrament!*" Matthieu exclaimed, launching into a tirade in French about how this would mess up the timing of the show and the group numbers. Bree looked to me for translation, but I just murmured to her that it would be okay, my arm tight around her shoulders.

I understood Matthieu's frustration, but I wouldn't let him make Bree feel bad. Before I could say anything, Theo came to stand at Bree's other side, interrupting Matthieu's rant, which was building steam.

"I have an idea!" Theo said brightly.

Stunned silent, Matthieu gaped at him. The

rest of the skaters did too. Matthieu wasn't the sort of guy people typically interrupted.

But Theo only smiled and said, "I'm dying to try out a new exhibition program I've been playing around with. I'd love to test it with an audience. I'd especially like to get your opinion on it. I didn't want to bother you. I know you have so much on your plate. Everyone's always asking you for help."

Matthieu pushed up his glasses, blowing out a long breath. "Well, yes. That's true. I suppose I could give you some notes."

"Really? That would be incredible. I'd owe you big time."

Head high, Matthieu made a little flicking motion with his fingers. "You're not getting paid more for doing extra routines, though."

"Of course not," Theo agreed. "You're doing *me* a favor."

Matthieu turned his attention back to Bree and me, his lips flattening. "I suppose you can do the group numbers alone, Etienne. I don't like not having an ice dance solo routine, but Theo's much more popular. So it's fine for today. Get better, Brianna."

With that order, he turned on the heel of his shiny leather shoes and strode off. Theo rolled his eyes, and the rest of the skaters gaped. Crouching in front of Bree, Theo gave her a smile, his cute dimples pitting his freshly shaved cheeks. He was gay, and if it wasn't for Sam…

How ridiculous was that? Sam was my best friend! Not into guys! Not into me! Maybe I *should* try it with Theo.

"Don't worry," Theo said to Bree, giving her hand a squeeze. "I'll handle that jerk. Rest up."

A tear spilled down her cheek. "Thank you."

Another skater said, "Wow. I was afraid he'd end up firing all three of you."

Theo scoffed. "I'm the reigning world champion. He's not firing me. And he needs an ice dance team. I wouldn't let him fire you even if he did try," he said to me and Bree. "My agent knows the billionaire who owns this place. Don't worry, okay?" He stood. "Now I just need to come up with a new show program. Suggestions?"

"You don't actually have one?" I asked, my voice rising and adrenaline spiking.

He shrugged. "I'll do a few back flips and shake my ass. Want to help me come up with something?"

As the cast put our heads together and tried to find a short song that would fit in with the show, Tim came to walk Bree back and put her to bed. I told myself it was a good thing Sam was off having fun with a pretty girl since I'd be way too busy in between shows helping Theo polish the new routine. Yep. It was a good thing.

Now I just had to believe it.

Chapter Five

Sam

I PACED THE hotel lobby under the gigantic Christmas tree. If there was an earthquake, that thing would be deadly. Not that there would likely be an earthquake. Why was I worrying about earthquakes?

Why was I worrying about anything? I was all tied up in knots for no good reason. Etienne had texted that Bree was doing better, and Tim had confirmed. Etienne had also said the shows went well, and now I was waiting for him so we could get dinner.

I'd told him to change into nice clothes even though I felt under-dressed in my jeans, Timberlands, and black sweater. The sweater was doing the heavy lifting, but Alice had assured me I looked fine for the hotel lounge. I'd checked my coat, and it was a little chilly every time people came and went through the wide revolving glass door.

I still felt weird taking the vouchers from her and using them on Etienne. But she'd insisted she was sick of the hotel's food and needed to get up early for work. She'd also mentioned that I'd talked about Etienne all day and clearly needed some "quality time" with him.

Which, yeah, I did. It was the whole point of this trip. She'd winked when she'd said it, so I guessed it was funny? I felt like my brother, who struggled sometimes to understand other people's humor. Maybe it was a Quebec thing.

Honestly, I was still pissed at Etienne. Snowboarding had been fun, and it had worked out since Etienne had been busy with the shows, but the way he'd been so eager to get rid of me that morning had bugged me.

Then Etienne was striding toward me in dark skinny jeans, leather boots, and a gray pea coat with red scarf knotted in a way I could never get to look good. He smiled—a real one, not a skating smile.

"Where's your coat?" he asked.

"Checked it. We're doing the lounge for dinner."

His eyebrows rose. "It's pricey, eh?"

"I've got an in with Alice. Don't worry."

"Ah, right." He smiled again, this one more of a grimace. "Where is she?" He gazed around as if expecting her to appear.

"Oh, she gave me vouchers for the lounge. She's at her place in the village."

His face weirdly blank, Etienne asked, "Did you go there?"

"The lounge? Not yet. It's just around the corner though."

"Alice's place."

"Oh. No, it wasn't like that. Snowboarding was dope, though. Guess if you want to get rid of me again, I can give it another try. Lift tickets are wild, but my parents would probably cover it."

Brows meeting, Etienne frowned. "Get rid of you?"

"Yeah." I shrugged. "You seemed really eager for me to hang with Alice."

"That's not—that wasn't for *me*. I didn't want to mess up your game."

"My 'game'? Dude, since when do I have game? I'm not—she was being friendly."

"Uh, yeah." Etienne fiddled with the tassels on the end of his scarf. "Because she's into you."

I scoffed. "Clearly not."

"That's classic you. In grade eleven, Sabrina Tate had to shove her tongue down your throat at a party before you got with the program. You don't have a great track record of knowing when people want you."

Looking away, Etienne's face flushed red. As I tried to connect Sabrina Tate to Alice, he cleared his throat and added, "She's hot. You should go for it. Don't you think?"

"Yeah, she's hot. I'm not saying she's not hot." My earlier irritation rushed back, and I worked to smother it. "This isn't about her. I came here to be with you, not pick up chicks. Why are you suddenly so invested in my love life? We haven't even played League yet. Hello, priorities."

He laughed weakly. "Right. I know. I just don't want you to be bored while I have to work." Closing his eyes, he rubbed his face. His thick lashes were dark on his cheeks. "I'm sorry. I wasn't trying to get rid of you. I'd never want that. I—" He shrugged. "I'm an idiot."

In a blink, my anger vanished. He was tired and stressed, and I was being an asshole. "I'm sorry too. Let's eat and have a few drinks. On me." I fished the vouchers from my pocket. "Well, the drinks are on me. Food's covered."

We checked his coat and made our way to the lounge. He wore a red sweater that hugged his lean, muscled torso, and I felt even more underdressed even though I wore a sweater too.

As we neared the lounge, Etienne's face exploded with so much joy that *I* stopped breathing and quickly caught up with him to see what he was looking at. A piano. Not a huge one, but not the backless kind we'd always had at home for my brother. A baby grand?

He stared at it like a kid on Christmas morning finding a new bike under the tree. Or a piano, I guess, since it was actually as close to under the massive, decorated pine in the lounge as possible.

"You should play it," I said.

The joy evaporated, his lips pressing together as his shoulders hunched. The brief flare of light in his eyes was gone as he shook his head.

"Why not?" I nudged his arm with my elbow, though not as hard as my grandma would. "Come on." I wanted the joy back. I wanted his eyes to glow. Not in a weird werewolf or vampire way—just with happiness.

He scoffed. "I'm so out of practice."

"Who cares? Do something easy." I glanced around the lounge. There were clumps of people on big leather couches here and there sipping from wine glasses and eating finger food. "A Christmas carol or something."

"I'm probably not allowed anyway." But he was still eyeing that piano.

"So they'll tell you to stop. Come on. I wanna hear…" I tried to think of a carol that might be easy to play, although I had no idea. Henry had all the musical talent in our family—I could do "Chopsticks." The end.

Granted, I'd only tried lessons for a month before insisting I hated it. Which I had. Henry was like a pig in shit spending hours and hours practicing a talent—either skating or piano. I guess Etienne was similar. I got bored too quickly. I still hadn't found the thing I loved enough to want to put in endless hours of work.

But one thing I loved a lot was seeing Etienne happy. My cheeks flushed hot. Not *loved*. Whatever. He was my best friend—nothing wrong with wanting him to be happy!

"You okay?" Etienne was frowning at me, his brows meeting.

"Yep. I want to hear…" I glanced around. "How about 'Jingle Bells'? That seems easy."

His lip curled with disdain. "I guess."

"What?" I laughed. "It's a good song."

"I said I was out of practice, not that I was seven."

I lifted my chin. "Go on, then. Show me what you've got."

Our eyes locked, and a strange silence drew out as we stared at each other. Why was my face so hot? I was challenging him to play the piano, not—

Not what?? Nothing! NOTHING.

Just before it got really weird, Etienne walked to the piano. I followed as my stomach flip-flopped. I needed to eat, clearly. He sat on the gleaming black bench, his spine perfectly straight. He ran his fingers over the keys, not pressing down yet.

It reminded me of when he took the ice before a performance and would stroke around the rink a few times, usually hand in hand with Bree. Here at the piano, he was alone. Should I sit beside him? Was he scared? I didn't want him to be scared. Maybe I shouldn't have dared him.

I was about to tell him it was okay and that he didn't have to play when he began a familiar-sounding song. It was one of those old Christmas carols I think I sang in choir in elementary school. Not "Silent Night," but similar. My brain whirred as I tried to place it.

Etienne's fingers danced, his wrists undulating. He swayed a little side to side, his posture still perfect. I was mesmerized. A lyric from the song filled my head.

Fall on your knees

The butterflies in my stomach flapped, and I had to be blushing even harder now. What was this? I didn't... Did I? With Etienne? With my best friend?

Why couldn't I tear my eyes away from him? Why did I...want? *What* did I want?

The gentle music rose and fell like it was controlling my breath. I stood frozen in place beside the piano, watching Etienne's profile. He had to be concentrating, but he didn't look like he was. His lips were parted and eyes hooded. Those thick eyelashes swept over his cheeks that were still pink from the cold.

The song—I remembered suddenly the name was "O Holy Night" or something similar—filled the air, and if this was Etienne rusty at the piano? I'd seriously not paid attention to how good he was.

It seemed effortless, like his fingers stroking the keys were magic. I'd watched him skate a ton, and it was a skater's job to make extremely hard moves look easy. He and Bree would glide along with the lightest smiles that masked the burn of lactic acid in their legs. Etienne was an expert at faking ease.

This was different. I felt like he really was relaxed as he played the song, seemingly lost in his own world that I wanted to be a part of.

I wanted to kiss him.

I wanted to kiss my best friend.

I wanted to kiss my male best friend.

Oh shit. What? Why? How? Since when? I didn't kiss guys. I'd never wanted to. Had I? Staring at Etienne play, I felt like my brain was leaking out of my ears. Because I definitely wanted to kiss him, and I guessed it didn't matter who else I did or didn't want to kiss.

Because no one else mattered.

I was about to climb on the piano and straddle

his lap so I could get my mouth against his when the song ended with a last echoing note. A new noise filled the air, and I realized everyone in the lounge was looking our way and clapping.

Good thing I didn't climb on the piano.

Etienne stood and nodded, giving the people a little smile. They all seemed genuinely impressed and not just being polite. I was struck with a memory of the first time our class in grade nine saw Etienne skate.

Some of the kids—especially the boys—had teased him when they found out he was a figure skater. Not just a skater, but an ice dancer, which sounded even more feminine to the assholes who thought skating was for girls.

It was actually how we'd become friends. I knew how hard and awesome skating was. I think I stood up for him one day? It was a blur now. He'd known who Henry was, and we'd sat together at lunch that day. And every day after.

Now, as I looked at the impressed faces in the lounge, I remembered the day our gym class went skating. How Etienne had *flown* around the rink going forward and back, spinning and weaving around the guys who skated okay from playing hockey but were clumsy next to him.

He'd won their grudging respect that day, and I'd been so proud of him. Pride burst out of me now, and I realized I was grinning at him. He returned the smile, hitching one shoulder in a shrug.

"That song's easy too," he said.

And shit, I still wanted to kiss him.

"Eat!" I blurted. "We should eat." I was so lightheaded it would be my turn to faint and get a concussion if I didn't get my shit together.

We found a pair of leather armchairs with a table between, and the server brought us appetizers and cocktails. He told me about Theo Sullivan stepping up to help and how everyone had pitched in to create a routine for him on the fly. I listened and smiled and ate little melted brie quiches and truffle fries.

And I still wanted to kiss him.

Fuuuuuuck.

AFTER PACING THE tiny cabin for too long, I tapped my phone and called Henry. It had been a whole night and day since I'd wanted to kiss Etienne. I'd barely slept, way too aware of his body so close to me.

I'd hardly breathed with longing. The bed had seemed smaller, Etienne *right there*, mumbling in his sleep as he'd shifted, his elbow brushing my ribs.

What was happening? Why was this temporary

insanity not going away? We'd hung out and played League, which I'd sucked at massively because I kept getting distracted by the way he bit his tongue when he really concentrated.

Bree was feeling much better, and Etienne was back at the arena with her for the evening show. I glared at Henry's pic on my screen. Why wasn't he answering? I redialed.

He answered, his very monochrome condo coming into view. He sat at his little table, eating what was very likely vegetables, fish, and either wild rice or quinoa or some shit. He turned the phone so it could lean upright.

I said, "Hey, bro. You're not at the rental house with the fam?" Like, obviously he wasn't, and some people might have replied, "*Duh.*"

Not Henry. He knew what I was really asking and simply said, "It was a long day at the rink. I'm taking an extra day off tomorrow." His black hair was damp, and he wore a gray sweatshirt. My brother was the handsome one of the two of us, and he always looked polished even after a shower.

"Hold on. You're taking an extra day off? You? Henry Sakaguchi? Do I have the right number?"

He ignored me as he sliced into whatever was out of frame on his plate. "The Ice Chalet is hosting a New Year's Eve family skating event that they need to prepare for, and it'll be open to the public over the weekend as well."

"So they're forcing you to take a three-day weekend for once?"

"Mn."

I laughed, leaning back against the decorated headboard, a Christmas light stabbing me under my shoulder blade. "Sounds about right. That'll be cool that you can spend more time with Obaachan and Mom and Dad."

He nodded as he chewed a small bit of what looked like salmon. I'm sure he had some home renovation show on HGTV paused on the TV. Another wild night for Henry. But who was I to talk? I was alone in a cabin in the mountains, still thinking about kissing my best friend.

Shit. Yeah, I was definitely still thinking about it. This wasn't working.

"Sam?" Henry watched me with a furrow of concern.

"Huh? Yeah, I'm here! Spacey as always. Awww, is that Esmeralda? Let me see her?" A calico tail had appeared in the corner of the screen.

Gently, Henry clucked his tongue, waited, then did it again and picked her up so she knew it was coming. She was fluffy putty in his hands, and he cradled her.

"Hi, Esme!" I waved as if she understood because I'm a dork. I was glad Henry rescued her. He seemed content with his routines, but I worried he was lonely.

"What's wrong?" he asked.

"Nothing!" Such a lie, but I wasn't ready to say, "*I want to bone my BFF.*"

Wait. What? I wanted to kiss him. Who said anything about boning? Well, I did, but…

I realized Henry was watching me patiently, nuzzling Esmeralda. She purred faintly. I shrugged. "Dunno. Do you ever wonder if you actually know what you want?"

He simply said, "No."

Fair, since Henry wanted to skate. He wanted to train, train some more, and win the Olympics in Calgary next season. Then probably keep training because he liked it so much more than performing. Oh, and he wanted to thrash Theo Sullivan in the process.

That reminded me. "Did you know Theo's here doing the show at the resort?"

Henry went very still, blinking at me. "Theodore's at Mont-Tremblant?"

"Yeah, apparently the owner of this new hotel's friends with his agent or something. He seems nice. Theo, I mean. No opinion on the hotel magnate or agent. I got to see the show the other night, and I talked to him for a while."

"Did he ask about me?"

I shrugged. "Sure."

"What did he ask?" Henry's gaze was like a laser cutting a diamond.

"Dunno. The usual small talk." Huh. Sometimes I wondered if Henry didn't actually dislike Theo underneath their rivalry. That maybe... Nah. I was overthinking.

"I'm sure he was tiresome." Henry bent out of frame and sat up without the cat.

I laughed. "He was cool. Anyway, Etienne and Bree are great." I paused. "It's been awesome catching up with Etienne. I missed him."

"Mn." Henry ate another bite of his dinner.

I missed him. It was true! It was no big deal. Yet now, that sentence felt huge. My face was hot, and I hoped the Christmas lights behind me hid it. Obviously I'd missed Etienne. That was totally normal.

Except now I want to kiss him.

Which wasn't *abnormal*, but... '

"What's wrong?" Henry asked.

I blurted, "Did you ever like girls?" *Smooth.*

"I like lots of girls."

"I mean as more than friends. I've always been into chicks, and I was just wondering if you were ever...confused. Or anything."

He tilted his head, regarding me with that serious expression that I swore could read my soul like a tweet.

#BicuriousBro

"Is this about Etienne?"

"What?" I squawked, practically falling off the

bed as I leapt up. "No! Why would you say that?"

"To begin, the way you're reacting to a simple question."

I groaned. I should have known better than to bring this up with Henry. I slumped back to the bed, my arm getting sore holding up my phone. "I thought about kissing him, okay? But we're best friends. It must be…" I cast around for anything. "The mountain air."

"Mn." Henry swallowed another forkful of his dinner. "Or perhaps you and Etienne have always had a deeper connection."

"What would you know about deep connections? You're terminally single." I winced. "Sorry. I didn't mean that." Ugh. I hated being mean, and Henry was the last person who deserved it. He was so kind. It was annoying sometimes.

He ate another bite and sipped his bubbly water before nodding.

I asked, "And wait—do you think this…*connection* goes both ways? You think Etienne likes me? As…more?"

"Possibly. Obaachan's always said so. She's usually right about these things."

My pulse raced. "You don't think it would be weird if Etienne and I…" I waved my hand. What? Hooked up? That thought sent desire ripping through me. Wow. Okay.

Got together? That thought made my heart go

boom.

"He's always made you smile like that."

"Huh?" I glanced down at the little square on the corner of my screen. Holy shit. I *was* smiling. Like a goof. Like a geek. Like someone with a crush. Except, was this a *crush* after knowing Etienne all these years?

"I don't think it would be weird at all," Henry said, eating the rest of his dinner and keeping me company on-screen while my head exploded, the whole world whipped off its axis, and I realized I'd wanted this for so, so long.

And now I had to spend another night sharing the same bed with Etienne without destroying our friendship.

Fuuuuuuck.

Chapter Six

Etienne

WHY HAD I thought the sauna was a good idea?

Sitting on the lower bench next to Sam, a foot or so between us, I stared at the fake rocks in the corner, rereading the sign in French and English warning not to pour water on the fake rocks in an electric sauna.

It was either that or look at Sam with only a towel around his waist. At least he wasn't licking a candy cane.

No! Don't think about that!

I only wore a towel as well, and if I let my desire bubble up, it would be disastrous.

"Okay?" Sam asked.

I glanced to my left. His eyes were closed, and he leaned back against the higher bench. He seemed completely relaxed, bare legs extended with ankles crossed tightly. Actually, Sam usually sat with his legs apart. Not extra wide like an asshole, but normally wide.

He cracked open an eye. "You're sighing a lot."

"Oh! Yeah, I'm fine." I whipped my head back front and closed my eyes. "Sorry. Tired, I guess."

"Don't be sorry. Doing two shows a day must be exhausting. This is relaxing, though." He was silent before adding, "Right?"

"Definitely."

Neither of us sounded sure. It should have been relaxing. That was the point of a sauna, though I'd honestly take a jacuzzi any day. I got hot so quickly in a sauna. Sam being almost naked next to me did not help.

"Etienne, I need to tell you something."

The hair on the back of my neck stood in a wave. I opened my eyes. "What's wrong?"

He sat up super straight, uncrossing his legs. His foot tapped restlessly on the wood planks. "Nothing's wrong. At least, I hope not?"

"Okay. Tell me."

He nodded. "I should. I should just tell you. You won't be, like, *mad* at me or anything."

My stomach twisted. "I won't. I promise. What's going on?" I waited for him to relax and tell me he was joking. About what, I had no idea. This didn't seem like Sam's usual humor.

With a creak and blast of freezing air, the door opened. A guy and girl wearing swimsuits hung up their coats and robes and put their boots beside ours in the tiny antechamber.

She said, "Sorry!" and they scurried in with towels, shutting the sauna door behind them.

Sam moved closer to give them more room, our bare, sweaty arms brushing. The spark that skipped over my skin was too dangerous. I blurted, "I think I've had enough," and Sam agreed. There was enough room for the four of us, but I'm sure the couple would appreciate privacy anyway.

And I had to know what Sam needed to tell me.

We said goodnight to them and squeezed into the antechamber to stuff our feet into our boots and throw on our coats. I had my bathrobe as well, and I offered it to Sam. I spent my life in ice rinks—I was used to the cold.

He smiled and wrapped it around himself before pulling on his coat. The more layers he wore, the better.

It was only about twenty seconds through the snow to reach the cabin. Bree and Tim's next door was dark. Sam and I went about changing into nightclothes and using the bathroom in silence. Was he going to tell me? Had he forgotten? Maybe it wasn't anything big after all.

Normally, we'd stay up later than midnight,

but I turned off the lights and climbed into bed. There was a strange hush between us that felt better suited to darkness. Sam slid in beside me under the duvet.

We hadn't spoken a single word since we left the sauna. Not even a goodnight. I could hardly breathe. Was he going to sleep without telling me? Should I ask? Was I being patient or seeming uninterested in him?

"Do you think it would be weird if I wanted to kiss a guy?"

For a second, I wasn't sure if Sam had actually said the words. Was I understanding? Did that sentence say what I thought? I'd grown up bilingual, but suddenly I felt like I didn't speak any language fluently. My heart was about to explode. My throat was a desert.

"Why would I think that's weird?" I didn't even recognize my own croaky voice.

I waited.

Sam was silent beside me. On our backs in the darkness, there was only a few inches between us. I stared at nothing, wishing I hadn't switched off the Christmas lights. Wishing I had the guts to turn my head to the right and look at him.

My muscles were locked, my body completely stiff. Including my dick. Was this happening? But what was *this*, exactly? Was Sam into me after all? Was he just talking? Wondering aloud?

I replayed his question. It hadn't sounded casual. His whisper had been quiet. Eager? Scared? I didn't want him to be scared. What if he liked someone else and was afraid to tell me? Even though the thought of him and another guy was a punch right in the balls, he was my best friend.

I loved him. I couldn't let him be afraid.

"It's okay," I whispered. "Whatever you want to do is okay. With whoever."

Silence. Aside from my raging heartbeat thundering in my chest. The heat from Sam's body beside me was a furnace under the duvet. Sweat prickled the back of my neck. If it wasn't me he wanted to kiss, I'd die.

It's not me! Stop dreaming!

When I'd asked him to come to Tremblant, I should have known there'd only be one bed. I should have known I'd be torturing myself for a week. *Joyeux Noël!* Happy New Year! Here's some torment!

"You don't think it's weird?" Sam's voice was unusually high.

I exhaled. "Of course not. I've wanted to kiss guys for years."

"Have you ever…"

My throat closed, my lungs frozen.

I waited.

"You don't want to kiss me, do you?"

It was still too dark to see him. Not that I

could move a muscle to look his way. I had to answer. But what was he asking? Was he freaked out? Had he finally guessed that I wanted him?

I should have gotten a cot from the hotel and given him the bed. Was I being a creep? Was all this because he was uncomfortable?

Wait. No, he'd asked about *him* wanting to kiss a guy. My mind circled out of control.

"Are you asleep?" he asked, barely out loud.

"No," I rasped. "I'm…" Speechless, apparently. Terrified? Dying? I had no idea which word was right.

The mattress between us dipped, his body shifting, making a shushing noise on the sheets. We still weren't touching, but we had to be only a sliver apart now. Sam's breath hit my cheek as he murmured, "Do you like me?"

This was it. After so long, here it was. *Yes. I like you the most. I love you. I've been in love with you forever. I want you like oxygen.*

I only said, "You're my best friend."

Sam made a little sighing sound, his exhalation tickling my ear. "Yeah. You too. That's not…" He went silent.

Was this really what it seemed to be? All signs pointed to yes. If Sam were anyone else, I'd have been kissing him already. I'd be on top of him, feeling the heat of his body under me, skin to skin.

I had to suck in a breath, my pulse hammering. I had to believe the evidence right in front of me. This wasn't idle talk. Plenty of times when we were teenagers, we'd had sleepovers and talked about life and the future and what-ifs and all that stuff.

This wasn't that. Sam was being brave, and it was my turn.

"I like you so much!" I spewed out the words so fast they slurred together. "I want to kiss you. If you want to kiss me, then we should."

"Holy shit. Seriously?" He sounded breathless.

"Yes."

"Okay. Should we… It's not a big deal. We can just…"

The bed dipped again, Sam rolling onto his side toward me as I rolled to him, and we finally touched. Not that we hadn't touched a million times over the years.

But not like this.

In the darkness, Sam's outline just visible, we pressed against each other. Through our T-shirts, our chests met, my flannel-covered knees poking his bare legs beneath his boxers. I snaked my arm over his waist, and his sweaty hand touched my neck like a brand.

Our fast little gasps were loud and hot as we sought with our mouths. We missed, and my lips found his chin as he hit my nose. Sam laughed in a high-pitched burst of warm air. I smiled as we tried again, joy bubbling through my veins like champagne.

Awkward and wet, our lips touched. Noses bumping. Another laugh. Mouths pressing. Finding the right angle. Third time the charm.

A real kiss.

I was kissing Sam. Sam was kissing me. We were kissing, and it was everything. I moaned into his mouth, pushing with my tongue. I shouldn't go too fast, but hunger gnawed. It was like when you didn't realize how starving you were until the first bite of food.

Sam moaned back at me like an answer as he opened for my tongue. We were kissing. This was happening, and it was perfect. Well, clumsy. I stuck my finger in Sam's ear as I reached up to touch his hair.

Still kissing him, I fumbled for the dangling cord of the Christmas lights. The extension cord was looped around a spindle on Sam's side, and I stretched over him blindly to plug in the cord.

Why was it so hard to get a plug in an outlet the right way? Maybe I'd ruin the moment, but I had to see him.

Under me now, Sam broke the kiss. "What are you—?"

The string of colored lights came to life. With Sam beneath me, I gazed down at him. His eyes were wide, lips wet, and face flushed. Or maybe it was the red and pink lights on his skin? I pressed kisses to his cheeks, and no, they were warm.

Pulling back, I met his eyes. He ran his hands up and down my back, and I pushed my knee fully between his thighs, feeling his hardness. My cock was iron against his hip, so he had to know I was turned on.

"Hi," Sam said.

"Hi."

He licked his lips. "Is this okay?"

I had to smile. "Yes." And I had to ask, "You really want this? With me? Not just because I'm here?" Did that make sense?

Apparently it did, since Sam nodded. "It's you," he said simply.

I dove for his mouth, ready to devour him, our tongues meeting desperately. My hips rocking, I moved on top of him, and he spread his legs for me like we'd been doing this forever.

For me. That's Sam's cock hard for me. He's kissing me. I'm kissing him.

I'd imagined this so many times, but reality was even better. Because I was tasting Sam's lingering toothpaste and inhaling his unique scent that was all him since he never wore cologne or aftershave since he barely had to shave.

Our groans were smothered as we kissed and kissed, rubbing our dicks through flannel. I was going to come way too soon. What if this was the only chance I got with Sam? What if this was one late-night experimentation because he was horny and we were sharing a bed, and he thought why not?

If this was it, I wasn't coming yet.

Gasping as I tore my mouth free, I pushed myself up on my arms, our groins barely touching now. Sam's eyes flew open, his brow furrowing.

"What? Why? Don't stop." He dug his fingers into my ribs. "Please."

"Don't wanna come yet."

"Oh, right. Okay. Yeah." His Adam's apple bobbed. "Good idea."

I shouldn't talk and potentially ruin this, but I couldn't help it. "Am I the guy you want to kiss?"

His frown returned, the furrow between his brows so cute. "Um, isn't that obvious?"

"I just thought maybe... Maybe you like someone else, but I'm here, so." I tried to catch my breath. I needed water.

"I'm not thinking about anyone else. Only you. I didn't realize it before. I didn't admit it. But this is all about you. There's no other guy. You're the one."

His fingers dug so hard into the tender flesh between my ribs that he'd leave bruises, and I lived for it. I kissed him fiercely before pulling back enough to whisper, "I want you more than anything. What do you—what should we do?"

He bit his wet bottom lip, and he was so cute I couldn't stand it. "What do you normally do with guys? I've only been with girls. I guess the principles are the same?" He laughed nervously. "I mean, friction and slipperiness. Holes. Um, filling them."

"Oh, Jesus. Yes. All of the above." I kissed him again, long licks into his mouth and soft moans, our pace slowing.

"What do you normally like?" he asked. "I think... You're a bottom, right? Based on stuff you've said over the years? About...wanting to be fucked? Liking that."

"Uh-huh." I nodded, rolling my hips against his and making us both moan. "But I'm verse. I can do you if you wanted? Have you ever been pegged or anything by a girl?"

He shook his head, his face definitely flushing in the soft, colorful glow of the lights. "I thought it was pretty kinky when Mandy started sticking her finger in my ass when she blew me."

I chuckled. "It felt good, though?"

"Yeah. You like stuff like that?"

"Hell yes. I love ass play. Fingers, tongue, cock, dildo. A banana one time when I was young and desperate."

Sam burst out laughing, his chest shaking. "You didn't! Oh my god. *When?*"

It was embarrassing, but this was Sam. He

knew almost everything about me. Now maybe *everything* since we were hard and touching and it felt so right. So natural.

"I was fifteen. Incredibly curious, but I wasn't ready for anything with another guy." *And I wanted you too much.* "It had brown spots and was getting soft, but was still hard enough. I thought maybe a dick would be like that. And I wanted to know, so…"

He still laughed, his fingers now circling my back seemingly unconsciously. "No way. You just stuck it in?"

"Covered it with a condom and lubed it up first with Vaseline. The internet taught me well."

"Wow." His laughter faded. "Did it feel good?"

"Not at first. It hurt. But I went slow."

Sam swallowed thickly. "Right. You must have been so, um, tight."

My throat was so dry. "Yeah. It was a little scary, but I kept going. Stretched myself."

"Did you get horny every time you saw a banana?"

Laughing, I nodded. "Lunch at school was a minefield for a few weeks."

It was so strange to be talking like this. Like we had a million times over the years—that was normal. But we were doing it in bed with our bodies pressed together and our lips puffy from kisses. And we were talking about my hole and stuff going in it.

"I really want your cock inside me." As Sam's eyes bugged out, I quickly added, "If you want to. No pressure. We can just do this. We can do whatever. I'm sorry. That was too much. I shouldn't have said that."

Sam smoothed his palms up and down my sides. "Don't be sorry. It's not too much. I... Can I... Do you have lube?"

As much as I hated moving off him, I forced myself up. I rooted around in my suitcase and yanked out a small bottle of lube and a few foil-wrapped condoms in a strip. Then I nervously chugged a small glass of water and refilled it for Sam. He drank half, and I returned the glass to the little kitchenette sink, almost dropping it.

Sam sat up on the bed, toying with the bottle of lube. I stood there, hesitating. I waited until he looked up at me to strip off my T-shirt. He licked his lips, watching as I stepped out of my PJ bottoms—and almost tripped as one leg got caught on my foot. I stumbled and landed on the bed, hitting Sam's legs under the duvet.

He laughed. "I thought ice dancers were supposed to be graceful?"

I put on a skating smile and hit a finishing pose, puffing out my chest. Sam golf clapped. "Nine for transitions."

I was naked and still hard, and we were laughing in bed, and somehow, I wasn't embarrassed. Then I was. Because I'd thought about it, and I shivered with anticipation and nerves, and I didn't even know what.

The duvet was bunched around Sam's waist, and he pulled it back for me, motioning me under. "Too cold." I crawled back to my side of the bed.

He seemed to think about it a moment before taking a deep breath and peeling off his T-shirt. Under the duvet, he squirmed, pulling off his boxers and tossing them to the floor. We sat up, naked with the duvet around our hips.

Right. Okay. I picked up the lube, fidgeting with the bottle. "So."

"So."

I was afraid if we sat too long thinking, it would get too awkward, and everything would be ruined. I leaned in and kissed him, figuring we could start there. Yes, good plan. Sam kissed me back, and we made our way down to the mattress, stretching out on our sides. Our tongues touched with soft, smacking spit sounds.

Soft smacking spit sounds. Say that three times fast.

I had to laugh, and Sam broke away, panting. He asked, "What?"

"Nothing. I'm just… Excited. Freaking out?"

He smiled tentatively. "Yeah. Me too. Is this

nuts?"

"No! We should keep going." *Please don't stop.*

"Right. Okay." He groped for the lube and popped the top. "So, if you like it, can I try…"

"Yes. Whatever you want to do." I nodded. "Uh-huh."

He smiled and squeezed a gob of lube onto his index finger. Watching me, he reached over my hip and poked around. I lifted my leg to help. "A little—there. Yep."

Biting his lip, Sam prodded my hole with his fingertip. He shifted his arm, trying to get the right angle. It was okay, but kind of awkward. He rubbed and asked, "Like that?"

"Almost. Do you want to… Hold on." I lifted my top leg and put my foot down by my right ankle on the mattress, making a sort of diamond shape. Holding his wrist, I squeezed lube on his middle finger as well, then guided his hand back to my ass.

Now he could reach easily between my legs. It felt like he used his middle finger to push in this time. The fresh lube was cold. There were other positions where my ass would be spread more—I could have gotten on all fours and pulled my cheeks apart for him to do whatever he wanted.

I moaned at the thought, pushing back against his tentatively probing fingertip. His eyebrows rose, and he pressed harder, circling my hole more confidently. It was better to do it this way so I could see his face.

So I could kiss him and murmur, "That feels good."

"Do you want, like, my whole finger?"

"Yeah." I moaned against his lips. "You won't hurt me. I want it."

"I guess after a banana, a finger's nothing."

We laughed. I said, "Well, and cocks tend to be bigger than fingers. Sometimes bananas, but sometimes not."

Sam crooked his finger, pushing and stretching me. "Would you want me to…?"

Our breath mingled where we faced each other on the pillows. I squeezed around his finger, and he gasped. It tickled my nose. I nodded and said, "I want you to fuck me. I want your cock in me. If you want to? Is this too fast?"

He thrust his finger in and out, circling my twitching rim. "I want to. I don't know what I'm doing, though. I mean, I've done it with girls, but not in the ass. Tried once, but she said it hurt too much."

"It's okay. We don't have to. It's the first time. I mean for us."

Us. It hit me again that I was actually doing this. I was kissing Sam, we were naked, and his finger was in my ass, trying to find my prostate. A burst of joy like fireworks spun through me.

"I want to," Sam said, breathing hard. "I'm so turned on. I think… I think I've wanted you for a long time, so it doesn't feel too fast."

I nodded. "I get it. I feel the same." Maybe it should have been strange to go from our very first kiss to penetration, but it was Sam. I was so comfortable with him. We used to share a tent and have farting contests.

How sexy to think about!

Grinning, I said, "Crook your finger. Like that—there!" He hit the right spot, and the fireworks exploded again, white bursts behind my eyes this time, my balls tingling and my cock leaking. "Jesus." I squeezed my hand between us to grab his wrist. "Get your cock inside me before I come."

He took out his finger, breathing hard. "Good plan. How?"

"Can I ride you?"

"Oh, wow," he whispered, rolling onto his back. "Yeah. That sounds good."

We worked together to get the condom on his cock and slick it, lube dripping into his pubes. He watched me take his shaft with wide eyes, his throat working and lips parting. I straddled him, sinking down as I reached back with one hand to guide him into me.

His cock was long and on the narrow side, and it curved a bit, stretching me beautifully. "So much better than a banana," I moaned, seating myself fully.

We laughed, and I loved him so much.

"You feel amazing," he mumbled.

I squeezed around him, making little circles with my hips. "Tight?" I wasn't a virgin, but I didn't hook up that much either. "You like it?" *You like me?*

"Yes. God, yes." Sam grabbed at my thighs, his fingers slippery. "I can't believe we're doing this."

"Me either. But I'm glad. Are you glad?"

I peered down at him anxiously. He was gorgeous in the multi-colored glow. I leaned my hands on his smooth chest, squeezing his cock inside me and never wanting to let go. If he wasn't glad—if he didn't love me back…

I knew in that moment my heart was on the line.

And because I was a freak, I asked, "Are you just horny? Am I really the one you want?"

Chapter Seven

Sam

GRABBING ETIENNE'S HIPS so hard I'd leave bruises, I tried to focus on what he was saying above the roar of lust and the urge to ram up into the incredible heat of his body.

"Yes."

Frozen on top of me, brows meeting, he asked, "Yes, you're horny?"

"I mean, yeah, but no." Holy shit, what were we even talking about? What was I saying? What were words? "Do you want me to sing *Grease* to you?"

Now he really looked confused. "Huh?"

A manic laugh bubbled out of me, and I crooned, "You're the one that I want." Fuck, I was a terrible singer. But I added the *oh-oh-oh* part as well.

"Oh!" Etienne's face lit up, that white smile gleaming in the rainbow glow.

"You're so cute," I said. "Have you always been so cute?"

God, he *beamed* at me. "I like to think so." He squeezed around me.

Grunting, I reached for his straining cock. I'd once exchanged hand jobs at summer camp when I was eleven with a boy whose name I now forgot, but this was most definitely nothing like that. I'd waved that experience off. A lot of kids experimented. It was normal. And it was! But I wasn't a kid now.

And Etienne was every inch a man. *Every inch, get it?* My brain lurched out of control as I stroked him. He wasn't huge, but his cock was hot and thick in my hand. To feel his excitement—his desire for *me*—throbbing in my grasp was incredible.

He closed his eyes, rocking into my hand and back on my dick as I thrust up into him. He'd always had such amazing rhythm, and I thought of earlier watching him play the piano and how I'd wanted to taste him.

We breathed hard, gasping and panting, our skin slapping. I muttered, "So hot. I want to kiss you." My brain coughed up words and phrases and my mouth released them.

Crying out, he came in long spurts all over me.

He squeezed around my dick, and I was so close, but I forced myself from the edge. I loved doing this when I jerked off—getting close and backing off, then again and again.

Panting in hot gusts, Etienne slumped over me, lifting off my dick. "Give me a second. Then you can…" He fumbled down for my shaft. "Sorry. You need to come."

"No rush. I like waiting."

Sitting up, Etienne slid back until he was across my thighs. He stared at my cock like it was, I dunno, a gold medal or something.

"Can I suck you?" he asked—like I'd say no.

"Um, *yeah*!" I peeled off the condom and tossed it.

We squirmed until he was between my legs instead of straddling them, and he ducked his head to—holy shit, swallow me to the root. So much for edging.

I couldn't stay still. I reached up with one hand, grasping at the headboard, about to levitate right off the bed. "Oh fuck, I'm gonna—"

Etienne pulled off my dick with a wet slurp that was absolutely obscene. Squeezing my eyes shut, I thought of guaranteed basic income—and fuck, it didn't help because I am really into GBI.

Also did not help even a little that Etienne was now kissing and biting and licking his way up my body. I kept my eyes shut. His weight between my legs and on top of me was amazing. He felt so much bigger than me, which was new. He was all lean muscle.

I liked it.

Then his face was in my actual armpit, which was extremely new. I wasn't too hairy overall, but I had sizeable tufts in my armpits. And Etienne was smelling me and rubbing his face there.

I liked it.

Was this a guy thing? I'd been with three girls before, and it had never happened. Was it an Etienne thing? Did he dig pits?

I liked it.

There was something raw and...*animal* about it. I thrust my hips up, dying for friction. I had to come. I tangled my fingers in his hair and begged. "I need you. *Please.*"

Etienne practically dove back down, his tongue teasing the head of my cock and Jesus, the suction and—

I snapped, unloading down his throat as I trembled and moaned. "Sorry!" I gasped, but he only groaned around my dick as he swallowed. I watched him lick and milk me, his mouth swollen and wet, his thick eyelashes seriously looking like eyeliner. He was gorgeous.

He's mine.

No idea if that would prove accurate, but boy did I like the idea. I petted his hair, closing my eyes as exhaustion swept over me, pleasure lingering. I was wrung out from head to toe.

I sighed as Etienne released my spent dick gently. The mattress lifted and water ran in the bathroom. I sighed again as a warm cloth wiped over the front of my body.

My brain did that weird, surreal thing it did when falling asleep, dreams forming. I slept, but I wasn't sure for how long...

Something brushed my cheek. Etienne's fingertips? I tried to open my eyes, but they felt glued down. This happened sometimes when I came really hard. Actually, I didn't think I'd ever come *that* hard.

"Sam?" His warm breath whispered over my face.

"Mm-hmm."

"Are you okay?"

"Uh-huh."

Silence. Then he said, "Please don't freak out."

The tremor in his voice had my eyes flying open with a spike of adrenaline. He was scared, and that wasn't okay. "I'm not. I promise. I mean, I am? But I'm not." I reached for him, my hand landing on his hairy chest. He was on his side watching me warily.

"Please don't regret it," he whispered.

I stroked my thumb over his coarse chest hair. "I don't." Did I? "No. I think my brain leaked out my ears, but I don't regret it."

He idly circled one of my nipples with his thumb. A fresh beat of lust that should have been impossible pulsed through me. I was too spaced to stop myself from moaning. His eyes shot to mine.

"You like that? Nipples?"

"Uh-huh."

For a while, he kissed and played with my nipples. It was shivery and delicious. I murmured, "When did you first start liking me?"

Etienne glanced up from where he circled my bellybutton. "A long time ago."

My chest tightened. I didn't know how to feel about that. Kind of weird, I guess? Flattered but also dumb for not realizing. How did I not see it?

I asked, "When, though?" I put on an arrogant voice. "Was it just my animal magnetism, or…?"

"Oh, yes. You were a beast at fourteen in your braces."

I laughed, but my heart skipped. "Wait, fourteen? When we met?" I barely stopped myself from asking, "*Was it love at first sight?*" No, I was not mentioning the L-word. Too soon! But maybe not for Etienne? That was *years* ago. Wow.

"You remember when I started at school? That first week, we were in gym class and Brad Douglas asked me why I'd moved to Vancouver without my parents. I guess it had spread around that I was living with another family. I was billeted at

Hannah Kwan's house since they had a spare room."

"Fucking Brad Douglas. I hate that D-bag. And yeah, I think I remember? Have you talked to Hannah lately, by the way?"

"Yeah, she and Anton Orlov are really coming along. I think they'll make the podium at Nationals in January."

"Shit, really? That's awesome. I'm out of the loop on pairs." I grimaced. "Ha ha, see what I did there?"

A sweet little smile lifted his lips. "I see." He leaned close and kissed me. For just a second at first, then deeper.

I threaded my fingers through his hair and opened my mouth, loving the slide of his tongue against mine, rough and wet and hot. Etienne was an amazing kisser. I was kissing Etienne. We were *naked* and kissing. The remnants of his cum had dried on my skin where he missed a spot with the cloth. My dick had been *inside him.*

Not just a guy, but *Etienne.* Who was kissing me and making my spent balls twitch back to life already, his tongue doing this swirling move that made me moan into his mouth.

This was so weird!

An incredulous laugh burst out of me, and as Etienne pulled away with his brow creased, I giggled uncontrollably.

"Um, what's so funny?"

"No, no, it's not." But I was laughing. "It is but it's not!"

He peered at me skeptically. "Are you high?"

"Only on fucking. Fucking you. I fucked you. We fucked." I motioned between us. "You and me. It's surreal."

Etienne smiled, still hesitant. "Yeah. I think I know what you mean?"

I drew him down for a laughing kiss. "It's awesome, don't get me wrong."

"Okay." He nuzzled my cheek.

"So, wait, finish telling me about when you first…" I motioned between us again. "Something about that asshole Brad?" *Focus, Sam.*

"Right." Propping his head on his hand again, he said, "Gym class. I told Brad I'd moved to Vancouver to train with a new partner. That I was a figure skater."

"Ohhh. I was just thinking about this, actually! I remember when we went skating as a class and you blew everyone away. And Brad had been a total prick about skating being for girls or some shit."

"Yup. I mean, I was teased a bit as a kid in the neighborhood, but I went to an arts school for piano. No one there had a problem with ice dancing."

"Henry got teased a lot. That's one of the

reasons he switched to homeschooling."

"I remember. People like Brad are everywhere. He thought it was hysterical that I was an ice dancer. He didn't even know what it meant, but it definitely sounded *gay* to him."

"Ugh. I hate that guy."

"And since I really was gay as well…" His gaze went distant. "It was scary. I remember that my shorts were too small. I'd transferred mid-year, and they didn't have the right size gym uniform for me. They had to order it, and in the meantime, I had to wear these shorts that were too tight."

"Huh. I don't remember anything unusual about your shorts."

He scoffed. "It was only one size too small— not a big deal. Like you said, people probably didn't even notice. But the elastic dug into me. I felt like everyone was staring. And I had an outbreak of zits on my chin." He shuddered. "Teenage nightmare."

"At least you never had braces. But yeah, I get it." Suddenly it hit me. "Oh my god! I remember this! The rope?"

He brushed back my hair, smiling softly. "Yeah. You heard Brad making fun of me for figure skating. And wait, why were you thinking about the time our class went skating and they realized I was an elite-level athlete?"

"It was when you were playing piano in the

lounge."

His brow furrowed. "Why?"

"Duh, because you're an elite-level pianist and you blew everyone away."

"What?" He screwed up his face. "As if. I haven't played in months. I'm so rusty."

"Could've fooled me."

"That's because you don't know anything about piano or music."

"Hey! I do too! Well, I have zero talent, but Henry played the piano too. I've listened to a lot of it and trust me—you've got the gift. It's special."

Etienne watched me suspiciously. "You're not just saying that?"

"Why would I? I already got you into bed."

Naked. In bed. With *Etienne*.

Fresh giggles erupted. Etienne joined in, laughing until he smothered my snickers with kisses. He rolled on top of me, and I spread my legs eagerly. Fuck, it felt so good.

And we were naked! We'd fucked, and all signs pointed to it happening again soon, and how was this real life? I was going to laugh again, but I managed to control myself.

"Wait, wait, you have to finish the story." I turned my face, dodging another kiss.

"You said you remembered."

"I still want to hear it." Heat flooded my cheeks. Was I being an egotist? Maybe, but it thrilled me to hear that Etienne had liked me for so long. It also made me feel like a blind fool, but I'd deal with that later. We were naked in bed, and I was happy.

"Happy" didn't start to cover it.

Etienne traced my mouth with his fingertip. "You marched across the gymnasium floor and informed Brad that figure skaters were incredible athletes. You said I was way stronger than he was. So he challenged me to a rope climbing race."

"Your shorts really were small. It's all coming back to me." I pictured him hauling ass up that rope, his lean, muscled legs long and arms straining. "I think... I think I thought you were hot."

His eyebrows flew up. "Yeah?"

"Yeah. But I locked that shit down fast. We became friends. Best friends. And I started going out with Sarah Zimmerman. But holy shit, imagine if you hadn't been able to climb the rope?"

He laughed. "I was definitely relieved. And Brad couldn't even get halfway up. It was extremely satisfying. He still mocked me, but..." Etienne shrugged.

Running my fingers through his chest hair, I smiled. "He was on his own after our class went skating. You were amazing, flying over the ice. You and Bree won the novice title the next year."

Sadness washed over him. "Yeah. And now…"

"It's okay." I rubbed his chest. How did it feel so natural? "You'll figure it all out."

He nodded, his thick lashes sweeping low as he kissed me. "So that's when. After you stood up for me. And gave me rope burns on my thighs in my short-shorts."

Laughing, I pushed him over onto his back. "Poor baby. I bet that hurt, huh?"

"It did!"

My heart pounded as I trailed my fingers down his hip. "Should I kiss it better?" Like, it had been years, so obviously his thighs were fine.

But I wanted to kiss him there. More than kiss.

Adam's apple bobbing, he nodded and spread his legs, and I was kneeling between them, eyeing his thickening cock. The shiny head poked out, and I bent to swipe at it experimentally. Etienne moaned raggedly, which sent all my remaining blood hurtling south.

Was I seriously doing this? Was I going to suck cock? And not just any cock—my best friend's?

His legs were dusted with dark hair, and I tentatively ran my hands over his quads, my thumbs dipping to his soft inner thighs. "Here?" I whispered.

Chest rising and falling, he nodded.

I ducked and pressed little kisses to the tender skin. He took my head, his fingers spread wide against my skull. But he didn't press or anything. I could feel the tension rippling through his body, but he just held me.

The girls I'd been with had all been shaved and waxed, so I wasn't used to all this hair. I think I liked it? I nosed at his balls, the hair tickling me, but I resisted laughing. I was going to suck cock, and I had to stay focused.

"You don't have to," Etienne murmured, apparently taking my slowness for hesitancy.

I lifted my head. "I want to. Really." His cock was fully hard now, and yeah, it was scary, but I was doing this. "I want you."

For a second, I thought he was going to cry. Then he nodded, biting his lip. He trembled with need and restraint, and fuck it. Time to just go for it.

So I did. I bent and sucked at the head of his cock, tasting bitter fluid. I grimaced, but no way I was spitting it out. I just needed to get used to it. Because I had a dick in my mouth, and I didn't hate it?

I had *Etienne's* dick in my mouth, and actually I kind of loved it.

Trying to remember the tricks girls had used on me, I sucked hard and fast, then slow. I explored with my tongue, pressing on the spongy flesh, spit dribbling out of my mouth. I stretched my lips wider and took more of him.

"*Tabarnak.* That feels so good."

I almost pulled off to ask if he meant that, but looking up at him under my lashes, I could see for myself that he was flushed and fidgeting, sweat gathering on his forehead. Yeah, he meant it.

I still had one of his thighs in hand, and his muscles twitched. After wrapping my other hand around the base of his shaft, I sucked up and down, twisting my palm. The noises were loud and embarrassing—but also hot. Fuck, it was hot.

Besides, I'd never judged the girls I'd been with for the slurping noises while giving a blow job—or the drooling. So fuck being embarrassed.

I was sucking Etienne's cock, and I was going to make him come as hard as I could even though we'd fucked less than an hour ago and he probably wouldn't be able to—

"Now, now!" He pushed my head, and I pulled off just in time for his cum to splatter my chin. I watched him, back arched and mouth open as he spurted every drop his balls had left. His eyes locked with mine, and fuck, I was so hard watching this.

I didn't even realize I'd started jerking myself until Etienne tugged me forward so I was up on my knees between his legs. Panting, he watched me, licking his lips.

"Come on me," he said hoarsely. "You're so beautiful. Wanted you for so long, Sam."

And even though we weren't those skinny kids in grade nine—the person naked in front of me was definitely a man—knowing he'd liked me all these years was powerful in a way that punched the air from my lungs.

To be loved more deeply than I'd ever known almost had me bursting into tears. Shit, I really was an idiot not to have realized.

I think Etienne loves me.

I think I love Etienne.

The orgasm ripped out of me, my jizz spraying Etienne's chest and belly. He watched me, moaning as if he was the one coming again. That he took such delight in *my* pleasure made my heart swell as my dick softened.

I collapsed on top of him, and we kissed and kissed until all we could do was laugh at how gross and sticky we were. He wiped at his jizz on my chin, then licked my skin clean, which was hotter than it had any right to be.

We jolted at a knock on the door and shushed each other, laughing like kids. I was giddy with joy and endorphins, and I grabbed Etienne's robe. I wasn't thinking about who might be knocking as I tied the terrycloth sash and opened the door.

It was the red pom-pom I saw first.

My grandma was under the Team Canada toque, grinning up at me. If she wasn't so cute, I'd have shut the door in her face.

Chapter Eight

Etienne

*B*REE'S GOING TO *know as soon as she sees Sam in my robe.*

Grinning at the ceiling, I waited to hear her familiar voice. Icy air blustered in from the open door, and I burrowed under the duvet.

"Obaachan! What? How? *What?* What are you doing here?" Sam's voice rose in clear panic.

I bolted up to sitting, then realized I was still splattered with jizz. Sam yanked the door halfway closed behind him, and I ninja-rolled out of bed, wincing as my knee cracked against the wood floor. At least the cabin was tiny, so I only had to crawl a moment before I was in the bathroom.

The tiles were freezing. I was naked. Sam's grandma was outside. Had I scrambled past the condom on the floor? Why hadn't I grabbed it?

Sam and I *had sex.*

"Focus," I muttered as I locked the bathroom door. What in hell Sam's grandma was doing on our doorstep, I had no clue. But the rest of Sam's family was likely here too.

I flipped on the light and turned on the shower. The only thing I could do at the moment was wash off the evidence that we'd just fucked.

Sam and I had sex. Sam likes me back. Sam might even—

I clapped a hand over my mouth to muffle the giddy laughter. I'd never been so happy, but I had to pull myself together. Under the hot shower, I scrubbed clean and pretended I was about to take the ice at a competition.

Stands full of people. Panel of judges ready to criticize every little angle of my blades and extension of my free leg. TV cameras rolling. Millions watching around the world.

With a towel around my waist since all my clothes were in the main room, I rolled my shoulders and put on my best skating smile.

Sam was still in the doorway, so I quickly pulled on sweats and a hoodie before joining him, smile intact. I gave Sam's family a cheery wave. They were all knee-deep in snow since the resort clearly hadn't shoveled the staff area yet and it had snowed again last night.

Sam's parents, grandma, and brother were

there, along with Bree, who watched me with very wide eyes.

I said, "Hi! What an amazing surprise!" *Smile, smile, smile.*

"My family's here," Sam said through clenched teeth.

"He has eyes, Samu!" Mrs. Tanaka opened her arms, and I stooped to hug her. Her parka was so puffy that she made me think of a snowman. "Happy New Year! We're going to see you skate."

"Awesome!" I straightened, still smiling as I hugged Sam's parents, then Henry. He smiled genuinely at me, giving me a little nod. Of approval? Had Sam told him?

Sam and I had sex. He likes me back.

"They were determined to surprise you!" Bree said. "But gosh, it's freezing out here! Why don't you two sleepyheads meet us for brunch in the hotel in twenty?" She made a shooing motion at Sam. "Your toes will get frostbite!"

Sam actually was shivering, and he blurted, "Yep, bye!" and practically dove back inside. I waved, still smiling, and closed the door.

"Oh my fucking god," Sam whispered. "Do I smell like sex? I must! Do they know?"

His panic sliced through me, hurting more than it should have. I understood why he was freaking out. Of course I did. But... Was he ashamed of me? Of being with a guy? Of being with *me*?

I said, "I don't know. We'll just act...normal." That word scraped out of my throat painfully.

Sam spun to face me. "Wait, that's not... I don't want to hide this. I don't want to hide you."

"You don't?"

"No!"

"I thought maybe you were freaking out, so..."

Sam ran his hands through his hair, making it stand up even higher. "Okay, yeah. I am. What we did was amazing. I loved it. I love—" He rubbed his face, breathing shallowly. "I don't regret anything, and I'm not ashamed of you. I just did not expect my family at the door while I can still taste you."

The hurt and fear faded like scratches on the ice smoothed over by the Zamboni. "That's fair. It's a lot to process. For me too. But I don't regret anything either. Not even a little."

We smiled at each other, moving into a hug. I loved being able to hold him so closely. We didn't slap each other's backs. No more fake bro bullshit. I breathed deeply.

"You really do smell like sex."

Groaning, Sam pulled free and tugged off the robe, dropping it on the floor as he disappeared into the bathroom.

Before long, we sat at a round table with Sam's family, Bree, and Tim. I gulped my coffee too quickly, burning my tongue. This was absolutely surreal. I felt like anyone who glanced at me and Sam would know immediately that we'd fucked. It had to be flashing over our heads in neon.

I looked at the menu, the words all blending together. I ordered eggs benedict because every brunch menu in North America had them. The server jotted it down on her pad, so clearly I was correct.

As the rest of the table chitchatted and our food eventually arrived, I managed to nod and smile. Under the table, Sam pressed his knee against mine. It was both comforting and unbearably erotic.

All I wanted to do was tell his family and everyone to leave us alone so we could have more sex. But Bree and I had two shows later, so I'd have to wait.

Tim said something I didn't hear, and Bree smiled at me, so it was probably a compliment about our skating. I nodded and gulped fresh coffee before remembering my tongue was burned. The hollandaise sauce had been soothing.

"*Tabarnak*," I muttered, then remembered where I was. "Sorry. Too hot." I motioned to my mouth.

"Did you burn yourself?" Beside me, Sam frowned in concern.

"You'll have to kiss it better, Samu!" Mrs.

Tanaka said with a wink.

All the air in the dining room whooshed out. My heart thundered in my ears. Was I wearing pants? This all had to be some strange dream. Everyone would be naked in a second. Not that I wanted them to be. Except Sam.

I asked, "Pardon?"

"Clearly you're romantically involved," Henry offered.

Sam choked on his mimosa, fidgeting as he managed to swallow. I stared at Henry, who watched Sam placidly. Henry typically said little, but he sure made those words count.

I glanced around the table. Bree and Tim sat frozen like they were watching a car crash. But Sam's parents were still eating. His grandma buttered a piece of toast. She chirped, "About time."

I had so many questions, but I waited for Sam. Swallowing hard, he looked at me before asking, "What do you mean?'

Mr. Sakaguchi stirred his coffee, the spoon clinking. "We always thought you boys might start dating eventually."

Sam only stared at his father with his mouth gaping. I said, "Uh, really?"

"Oh, yes," Mrs. Sakaguchi said. "You seemed keen on our Sam for ages."

"I... Yeah, I was."

Bree exclaimed, "I knew it!" She shared a satisfied smile with Tim, who nodded.

"We all knew it." Mrs. Tanaka pinched Sam's waist, and he yelped, jerking sideways on his chair and almost ending up in my lap. "Just took this birdbrain a while to catch up."

"He's not a birdbrain!" I insisted. The Sakaguchis *awwwed* in unison.

Mrs. Tanaka winked at me. "I always knew you were a good boyfriend."

"So…" Sam shook his head. "You figured out I'm bisexual before I did?"

"Yes, dear," his mother said. "Well, of course we didn't *know*, but we thought there was a good chance."

"I knew." Mrs. Tanaka took a big bite of crispy toast, crumbs sticking to her lipstick. "You were too stubborn to listen."

"Wow," Sam mumbled. "So, this is a thing that is happening in real life."

Bree lifted her glass of water. "To Sam and Etienne. Finally!"

They toasted us with champagne flutes and coffee mugs. I lifted my mug and shared a smile with Sam, counting the minutes until we were alone again.

THERE WERE WAY too many minutes until Sam and I were together.

After two shows and a late dinner with Sam's family, we were finally back in the cabin. I pulled off my boots and brushed fresh snow from my hat and coat. Sam hung up his coat and fidgeted, removing his socks. Then he apparently decided the cabin floor was too cold and tugged them back on.

I was dying to kiss and touch him, but I held back. He seemed agitated and had been quiet at dinner. Was he regretting this? Regretting *me*? There was only one way to find out. I'd spent too many years staying silent about my feelings.

"Are you sorry?" I asked.

By the microwave, Sam turned to frown at me. "For…my family showing up unannounced?"

I shook my head. "About this." I motioned between us.

"Why would you think that? Are *you* sorry?"

"No! Not at all."

"Me either." His brow furrowed. "So what are we talking about?"

"I don't know?" I laughed as the stupid stress released.

"Shouldn't we be making out?"

"Absolutely."

It was still strange to reach for Sam and kiss him. To have him kiss me back eagerly, slipping his tongue in my mouth and tugging at my clothes. For Sam to get us both naked so we could crash onto that wonderful bed and kiss and rub and get off with hands and mouths.

It was the best kind of strange I'd ever known.

Under the Christmas lights, we dozed, tangled together. I groaned drowsily after a while. "Need to sleep for real. I ate too much. Again. Those red pants aren't going to fit."

Sam rubbed my belly. "You can gain a pound or two. It's fine."

Imagining what Yaroslav would say about *that*, I squirmed away and stood. "It's not. But I really should go brush my teeth and get to sleep. I was dying by the end of the show tonight. Training's going to be brutal next week."

Still naked, I pissed and brushed my teeth in the bathroom. Sam appeared in the door wearing his boxers, his arms crossed over his bare chest as he watched me.

I spit into the sink. "What's up?" Something was.

"You got all tense and stressed."

I gulped a glass of water and spit again. "Sorry. It's not you."

"I know. It's Hackensack. It's your asshole coach." He paused. "It's the obsession with the Olympics."

I tapped my toothbrush on the side of the sink

too hard, defensiveness rising. "I'm not *obsessed*. The whole point of skating is to make the Olympic team."

"Um, is it, though? Do you *have* to go to the Olympics?"

I stared at him. "What do you mean?" My heart raced uncomfortably. I didn't want to talk about this. I wanted to go back to bed and sleep with his breath on my skin.

He raised his hands. "I know it seems like I'm suggesting treason or… What is it when it's against religion? Heresy? What I mean is—does the success of your skating career have to involve competing at the Olympics?"

I opened and closed my mouth. "Of course."

"Okay. I know my brother's answer would also be a resounding *yes*. But why? It's one competition. Is it really so different from going to Worlds?"

"Yes! It's the *Olympics*! It's everything we've worked toward for all these years! Without it…"

"Without it, what?"

"Nothing. It's the pinnacle. The purpose."

"But only three ice dance teams max get to go. Every four years. And next season there'll be two spots barring some kind of miracle. There are dozens of you working your asses off for your whole lives. Hardly any of you will actually make it to the Olympics. So does that mean all of your careers were for nothing?"

Yes! That was the immediate answer that screamed in my mind. Yet I knew everything Sam was saying was true.

"I don't want to piss you off. But I have to say this." Sam blew out a big breath. "If you don't go to the Olympics, that'll suck. You'll miss out on an extremely cool experience. I'm sure it's exciting and fun to be in the Athletes' Village and walk in the opening ceremony and all that stuff. It's a huge event. It would be dope to go."

I nodded. "It would be the biggest moment of my life."

"Would it, though? You've accomplished so much already. You and Bree are the fifteenth best ice dance team in the whole *world*. You've been on the national podium twice with a silver and a bronze. You've won and medaled at a bunch of international competitions."

I scoffed. "Not on the senior Grand Prix circuit. We've only won B competitions and junior stuff."

"Right, you won the whole Junior Grand Prix Final that one year. That was huge."

"But it doesn't matter if we don't succeed as seniors!" I paced back and forth in the tiny bathroom, my fingers twitching.

"What's 'success' really mean? You're already more successful than most competitive ice dancers in the world. I grew up around skating. I've watched Henry compete for years against other skaters who never won a national senior medal. You have two."

"Not gold!"

"So, if you win the Canadian title, that will make you successful? If you go to the Olympics and place fifteenth, will that be good enough? Or will the bar go up? There will always be more you can achieve, but why do it if it makes you miserable?"

I stumbled. "Miserable?" It was like my darkest secret was being exposed. Even though it wasn't a secret, was it?

"Um, yeah? I don't think you've been happy skating in a long time. Definitely not since you and Bree moved to New Jersey. You live so close to New York City, but you've barely visited since you have no money or time. Or energy. You escape into video games with me and then every morning you go back to that rink that you hate."

I could only stare at him. This wasn't a conversation I was prepared for. But I hadn't been prepared to have sex with him last night or to come face to face with his family this morning. My life was changing radically. I had to keep pace.

"Maybe I should shut up, but I love you too much not to say this," Sam blurted, his eyes widening. "There's no point in hiding it or pretending, right? Not now. I'm saying all this

ONLY ONE BED

because I love you, and I want you to be happy.
Yes, I think you're miserable. I think you and Bree
hate it in New Jersey. You feel like you have to
train with the best coach to succeed, even if he
barely spends any time with you one-on-one. Even
if it's insanely expensive and you don't have fun at
the rink like you used to."

I could barely speak. "Is that all?"

"No. I think you made the choice between
skating and piano at fourteen when you left home
to train with Bree across the country. You don't
think you can do both and succeed. So you picked
skating because you *did* love it. You still do deep
down even if it's making you miserable now.
When you played the piano in the lounge, that
peace and joy I saw on your face? That's what
skating should be too. Yeah, of course training is
hard, and nothing is all good all the time. But you
don't need to try for the Olympics if you don't
really, really actually want to."

My chest heaved. I saw white spots.

Sam lifted his arms and let them fall. "Okay.
Cry or yell at me or I dunno what."

All I could do was lunge for him, lifting him
off his feet as we kissed. He loved me. Not just as a
best friend. And he loved me enough to tell me
what I had to hear. Sam moaned in relief, opening
his mouth for my tongue, and throwing his arms
around me.

He was my home and safety and comfort and truth. "I love you," I gasped against his lips as we stumbled out of the bathroom.

On my back in that perfect bed, I opened for him the way I had in my fantasies. He fucked me tentatively at first, then with growing confidence as we kissed and clutched each other. Had it only been twenty-four hours since the first time?

I supposed that was another truth I had to accept even though it felt like I'd been kissing Sam forever.

BREE TEASED ME about Sam on the walk to the arena and as we laced our skates. She was thankfully having a good concussion day. We were early and alone at the moment, and I laughed along with her as we sat on one of the benches backstage in our stretchy warm-up clothes.

My mind ran over what I had to tell her like I was rehearsing a speech. What I wanted to tell her. What I was terrified to tell her.

I knew she didn't like it in Hackensack. Still, butterflies flapped in my acidy stomach. Maybe I should wait. Tomorrow was New Year's Eve. We'd only have an afternoon show, and then we could celebrate with Tim and Sam. Was I going to ruin that?

Was I going to ruin *everything*?

"Come on." She stood and poked my shoulder. "You have to let me gloat about knowing you and Sam were into each other. I admit my victory is tarnished by the Sakaguchis and Mrs. Tanaka also knowing, but still."

I tried to smile. "Gloat away."

Her grin vanished. "What is it?"

"Will you hate me if I want to quit?" There it was. Out in the world.

For a terrible moment, Bree stared down at me, frozen. Her face crumpled. In a heartbeat, she choked on a sob, tears already falling. "I was afraid you'd hate *me* for wanting to quit."

Eyes burning, I jumped up and drew her into a fierce hug. "I could never hate you."

For a minute, we just held each other and cried. It was long overdue. Then Bree mumbled something against my neck. My skin was damp with her tears.

"Hmm?" I asked.

She lifted her head, sniffing loudly. "I'm not sure I really want to quit, though. Are you?"

"I don't know." I ran my hands up and down her back the way I did when we were waiting to perform. It was our little routine, to look into each other's eyes with her arms looped around my waist. She did it now, probably an automatic movement. We breathed together.

Her voice was steadier as she said, "I want to quit because I don't love skating anymore. I used to love it so much. But I haven't since we moved to New Jersey."

A breath punched out of me like I'd tripped and hit the ice. "Me either. I hate it there."

"Right?" Eyes wide, she stared at me. "I know we're supposed to be grateful Yaroslav took us on, and he has all that pull with the judges, and even if he barely pays attention to our skating, if he's with us in the Kiss and Cry, it matters. But I hate it."

I'd nodded along as she spoke. "Yes. Yes! I hate it. Svetlana's fine, and I know it's good to train with the best teams in the world, but the atmosphere at the rink makes me feel shitty."

"Yaroslav calls me 'Deanna' half the time if he even deigns to pay attention. We knew we wouldn't be his priority, but I miss having a coach that genuinely cares about us."

"Me too. He's an expert on technique, but... It used to be fun. We laughed. We can work hard and still laugh sometimes."

"Right?" She squeezed my waist eagerly, bouncing on her toes. "We laughed all the time at Mountain High."

I thought of our old training center in Vancouver wistfully. "Do you think..." Was this a terrible idea? Or maybe... A bolt of excitement shot through me.

"I called Laura yesterday." The words tripped out of Bree's mouth. "She said we can come back." Fresh tears spilled from her eyes. "She was so kind. She always understood why we left, and she said we can always come home." Her voice broke. "I want to go home."

We clutched each other in another hug, crying again. Through my sniffles, I said, "Let's go home. Let's love skating again. And I want to take piano lessons." I drew back to look at her. "I miss it too much."

She nodded hard. "Absolutely. And if we keep training for the Olympics, and we don't make it, that's okay. It has to be okay or we should quit now."

I forced a shuddering breath. Could it be okay to not go to the Olympics? Could we keep training because we loved it? Could skating be fun again? Could I take time to play piano and not live and breathe training every minute?

"We should try." My words were shaky, and I swallowed hard before repeating them. "We should try. If we want to quit at the end of this season, we will. And it'll be okay. But we should go back to Vancouver. We'll take it slowly with your concussion. You can take off as much time as you need, and it'll be okay."

She wiped her eyes. "Yes. And I'm moving in with Tim."

"Maybe I'll move in with Sam." I said it without thinking, but the words sure sounded good.

Bree grinned. "After all, you two have been dating for years. You just didn't realize it."

I bent to pick her up in another hug, her feet off the ground. I would have spun her, but spinning was better left to our performances. My chest was light, a weight I hadn't wanted to acknowledge gone. We were going back to Vancouver and a coach who cared. And Sam.

We were going home.

Chapter Nine

Sam

WHY HAD I thought the sauna was a good idea?

Because Etienne needed to unwind after another evening show. Because his gorgeous muscles were tense. Because I enjoyed torturing myself?

Though I did enjoy stretching out the anticipation, knowing we were going to fuck as soon as we were back in the cabin. Knowing we loved each other. Knowing we could have a ton of fun making up for lost time.

"I've been thinking," Etienne murmured, his eyes closed. He sat in only a towel, his worn robe hanging off the bench beside him.

"Yeah?" I failed pathetically at sounding casual. I knew he'd heard what I'd told him last night, so I hadn't brought it up again today. It was his decision in the end.

"I'm thinking about bending you over this bench and eating your ass."

I just about hit the ceiling. My towel tenting, I suddenly found it hard to breathe. "That sounds… Um. I'm not mad at it."

Eyebrow arched, Etienne cut a glance down at me. "Evidently."

"Like you're not hard under that robe that is suddenly over your lap?"

"Oh, I am. Very hard. Thinking about how good I'll make you feel. What kind of noises you might make when I lick right inside you."

I shuddered in anticipation. "We can't. Someone could walk in any second."

Etienne sighed. "Sadly. It would be irresponsible. I have a reputation to maintain. Sauna sex scandals do not play well with Olympic judges."

My heart skipped. "You're worried about Olympic judges in particular? Are you and Bree going to go for it?"

Etienne exhaled. Sweat dripped down his temple, and I wanted to lick it. "What would you think if we kept training and tried for that spot next season? Assuming we still want to after the rest of this season. If Bree's well enough and we're not miserable."

"If that's what you want to do, I'm with you all the way." I hated to think of him slogging through another year plus at Hackensack since he was so unhappy there, but of course I'd support him. No matter what.

He snagged my hand, pressing his bare knee into mine. "What would you think if Bree and I moved back to Vancouver to train?"

Again with the hitting the roof. I bolted straight up, gripping his fingers. "Seriously? You want to come back? To train with Laura?"

Etienne nodded, his breathing shallow. "We want to love skating again. We want to be happy at the rink every day. Laura said she'll take us. Bree can move in with Tim, and you and I can—" He broke off. "If you wanted? Unless it's too fast. Is it too fast?"

I yanked him into a kiss, sweeping my tongue into his mouth and swallowing his yelp. He kissed me back, and we didn't need words since our mouths were too busy. And kissing in a sauna wouldn't be a scandal if someone caught us, right?

Okay, by the time I was straddling his lap, rocking against him with my towel falling off, we were definitely in scandal territory even if his tongue wasn't in my ass.

Breaking the kiss, I gasped for air in the thick heat. We were slick with sweat, and I did lick the side of his face before kissing down to his throat. I sucked his fevered skin as he dug his fingers into my spine.

"For. The. Record," I bit out between kisses. "It's not too fast. We had years of foreplay. We should have done this ages ago. What were we waiting for?"

"Can't remember now. Stupid, huh?" He grabbed my ass, grinding me down against him, only terrycloth in our way.

Laughter echoed outside, and I ended up on the sauna floor. By the time my towel was knotted shut and Etienne was checking me for injuries, the voices had faded.

It was our turn to laugh as we opened the sauna, yelping at the freezing air and jamming our feet in our boots to run back through the snow to our cabin and warm up again.

And get Etienne's tongue in my ass. And look up apartments in Vancouver. And *laugh*.

EYEING THE ICE trail in the dusk, the colored fairy lights strung along it ready for Instagram, I shook my head. "Is this the best way to spend New Year's Eve?"

Etienne waved an arm as he spun in a circle, his blades skimming the ice so smoothly he could have been levitating. "Mountains, ice, forest, friends. Sounds perfect to me."

"Because you skate for a living." I tugged down

Obaachan's borrowed toque, and Etienne bopped the pom-pom on top. His hat was red too, and I kind of loved that we matched. Were we one of those nauseating couples?

I sure hoped so.

"See?" Etienne said. "You're smiling now. Come on. Skate the trail with me. I'll warm you up after."

Desire tugged low in my belly. It had only been a few days, and I knew we'd get tired of fucking like bunnies, but... Not yet. I faked nonchalance. "We're eating a late dinner with my family later."

He sighed dramatically, dropping his arms to his sides. "True. I guess we'll be too tired to do more than kiss at midnight." His shoulders stiffened, and he seemed suddenly nervous. "Not that you have to. In front of so many people, I mean."

Bending my knees, I pushed on my right blade, intending to glide the few feet between us. I moved a few inches, and panic set in as I wheeled my arms. He grasped my shoulders, chuckling.

"Hold my hand. You're a terrible skater, so no one will think..." He shrugged.

I guess neither of us were used to being a couple in public. Taking a deep breath, I inched forward on my blades and kissed him. Not a peck, but not an inappropriate public tongue bath either. A good, solid press of our lips.

Our breath plumed white in the winter air as we parted. I asked, "What about now? Will everyone think you're my boyfriend?"

Etienne bumped our noses together. "They can't miss it." He glanced around at the people starting the trail around us in a stream of colorful scarves and hats. "Good thing they can't read my mind, eh?"

Behind me, Bree laughed. "Uh, your mind is very transparent, just so y'know." She held Tim's hand as he took choppy strokes beside her.

Henry glided up and nodded to us, his eyes gleaming as he looked down the trail. I was glad he'd get a chance to skate even though he should have been taking a complete break from the ice.

Theo appeared with a friendly wave. He called out, "Hey guys! This trail is awesome!" He squinted into the distance where the ribbon of ice curved into the forest, the colored lights reflecting on the fresh mounds of snow. "Not *too* many people. We should race."

The words were barely out of his mouth before Henry was off, his long, graceful strides building speed instantly. Theo sputtered and chased him, bending low.

Bree shook her head. "They need to sleep together and realize they're secretly in love. Like you two!" She winked. "Not that it was much of a secret."

"It was too!" I insisted. "I had no idea!" Grumbling, I took Etienne's hand, our leather gloves squeaking. I inched forward with tiny little steps, watching Bree and Tim skate off. Henry and Theo were long gone in their own little world.

"We're going to skate," Etienne said. "Not walk on the ice."

"Are we, though?" I bent my stiff knees.

"That's it! I won't let you fall."

Holding Etienne's hand, I trusted him the way I always had. He was my best friend. Even if we fell, we'd do it together.

THE END

Will Henry and Theo sleep together and realize they're secretly in love?

Find out in *Kiss and Cry*!

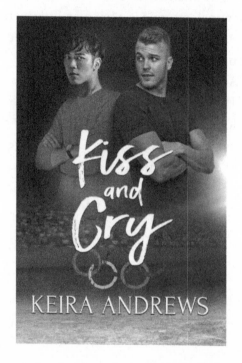

Will enemies become lovers while fighting for gold?

Henry
Everything comes easily for Theo Sullivan, whether it's jumps or figure skating world titles. Everyone loves him—judges, fans, coaches.

I hate him.

Now he's invaded my training center, and I have to see him every day as we prepare for the Olympics. I'm going to win gold if it's the last thing I do. I'm going to beat him.

But the strangest thing is happening. I'm peeking under his happy-go-lucky exterior and discovering there's more to Theo than I imagined.

This is a mistake. I can't trust him.

I can't be falling in love.

Theo

My mom's convinced training with Henry Sakaguchi will distract me heading into the Olympics. No way—Henry's epically boring and cold. He might as well be carved from ice.

But when I need help, he's there. He tries to keep me at arm's length, but it's no use. He's too kind. Too generous. He's caring and gorgeous and *hot*, and I've never wanted anyone like this.

I might want Henry more than a gold medal.

Am I falling in love?

Kiss and Cry by Keira Andrews is a steamy gay sports romance featuring opposites attracting, enemies to lovers, secretly soft-hearted boys, hurt/comfort, and of course a happy ending.

Keep reading for a sneak peek:

H OURS LATER, I'D escaped the competition banquet after making my obligatory appearance. It was a damp, drizzly night, which was the norm for Vancouver. After putting on sweats and lacing up my shoes, I slipped out of the hotel and ran down to the seawall and along the path there, replaying my free skate and itemizing the mistakes I'd made.

In the hotel lobby, I sped to the elevators with my head down and hood raised. The banquet had surely ended by now, but plenty of people would have spilled out into the bar. I kept my eyes on my mud-flecked shoes until I stepped off on my floor, relieved at the hush that greeted me.

A hush demolished by Theodore calling out, "There you are!" and flashing one of his smiles.

He loitered by my room, so I had no choice but to approach. Leaning one shoulder against the wall, blue dress shirt hugging his lean torso and suit jacket slung over his shoulder, he asked, "Can you do me a favor?"

No. "What?"

"I lost my card." He seemed to read my mind. "And my phone's dead. Can you call down for me? My room's just down the hall."

It was preferable to spending any more time with him than necessary, so I nodded. And then he followed me into my room because he was insufferable. Also, clearly intoxicated judging by his bright eyes and slight stumble.

"I have to piss. Can I?"

"Presumably."

He laughed, tossing his jacket onto the wooden desk chair and missing by a mile. "See? I knew you were funny under all that seriousness."

"I'm not."

This only made him giggle and hiccup. "Sorry. I had too much wine. Or cocktails. Or maybe both. You should have stayed. There are lots of Russians here, and they know how to let loose."

Ignoring him, I dusted off his jacket and hung it over the chair before calling down to the front desk. They agreed to send someone up with a key, but of course had to see ID before handing it over. I'd forgotten to ask him his room number, and the receptionist wouldn't tell me, so they'd come up to my room.

Which meant I was still stuck with Theodore.

He emerged from my bathroom talking as if we were in the middle of a conversation and *flopping onto my bed*. "So I dared them to shoot tequila instead of vodka."

I had to be dreaming. He was not really here in my room with his dress shirt now unbuttoned down to his chest and hanging out of his trousers, his tie unaccounted for. Sprawled on the bed I'd been using. Still wearing his leather dress shoes. Dark chest hair peeking out of the wide collar of his aforementioned shirt.

On. My. Bed.

He gave me a dazed smile. "Don't you think?" When I didn't answer, he added, "That the Russian ice dancers aren't as good as that new hot Italian team, but they'll probably win anyway. And they can hold their tequila surprisingly well."

"Your shoes are on my bed."

"Oh. Sorry!" He looked at his own feet as if surprised to see them. "I figured you'd take the bed by the window. It's funny how most of the rooms at this hotel have two beds even if you ask for only one. I used to get a roommate to split the cost, but I made great money touring Japan last spring. But you know, these coverlets are probably covered in jizz, so don't worry about shoes."

Correction: this had to be a nightmare.

He bolted up to sitting. "Not my jizz. I didn't, like, jerk off on your bed." He laughed. "Wait, you were in here, so you know that. You would have seen me jerking off. Not that you would have just watched."

Our eyes met, and his laugh faltered. My face was hot.

His Adam's apple bobbed, and he laughed again. "What I mean is, I saw this thing on TV where they brought one of those UV lights or whatever—like they use to find blood splatter that's been cleaned up—and they examined hotel rooms and the bedspreads don't get washed very often and it was cum city."

Which was disgusting, but hearing him say "*cum*" sent entirely inappropriate desire bolting through me. Glancing around the room, I had to look anywhere else but at his parted thighs.

"Gross, right? The remote is apparently super germy, which makes sense."

He rattled off more repulsive facts, and though I'd known hotel rooms weren't as clean as I'd like them to be, they'd been a staple of my life for years. I hadn't wanted to think about it. I'd taken off my running shoes by the door and now I was glad to be wearing socks on the carpet.

"I need to shower," I blurted.

Theodore's gaze dragged up my body. "Oh, right. You were running. Why didn't you stay to celebrate?"

I spat the word like poison. "*Celebrate?*"

"Yeah. I mean, I know you came second, but..." He winced. "Sorry. I shouldn't have brought that up."

"Neither of us has anything to celebrate. We're lucky the rest of the field was weak."

He shrugged. "It wasn't my best, that's for sure. But I still won. And I won Skate America last week, so I'm through to the final for sure. That's definitely worth celebrating."

"But you were sloppy. Your transitions were

barely there. If you'd show up to practice on time and do your run-throughs and stop being lazy, you'd—" I broke off. Why was I trying to help him?

With an eye-roll, he said, "Yes, *Mom*. I still beat you."

I clenched my jaw at the reminder. "Don't you care that you didn't perform as well as you could?"

"Why do *you* care? It's not very killer of you."

I had no idea how to respond to that. He was laughing to himself in that way drunk people did sometimes.

Apparently my confusion was evident because he said, "Oh, I mean you're supposed to have the killer instinct. My mom is always praising how ruthless you are." He wrinkled up his face. "But I dunno. You could have left me in the hall, but you're helping me. Here I am." He motioned to himself and the bed. "I don't think you're as cold as people say."

It hurt, but only a twinge. I'd much rather everyone thought I was ruthless and steely than betraying the truth about my weakness. I said nothing.

Theodore eagerly filled the silence. "Anyway, it's done now. No point in beating myself up about today. Who cares about one Grand Prix event? It was good enough. It's the Olympics that matter."

Good enough? Who cares? I clenched my fists, a tide of fury rising. How could he not *care?* He could be truly great—perhaps the greatest of all time—if he put in the effort instead of the minimum. With his natural talent, he'd be unbeatable. He almost was already. It was such a *waste*.

"Do you care about anything? Don't you want to make Mr. Webber proud?"

Face paling, his smile vanished. He opened and closed his mouth. "I…"

Then Theodore shot off the bed and into the bathroom. I listened to him vomiting, guilt washing away my resentment. I considered bringing him a bottle of water from the mini bar, wondering whether it was better to try and help or give him privacy and not intrude. Even though it was my room.

In the end, I was still debating when he emerged, red-faced with his hands in his pockets. "Sorry. Tequila was a bad idea. I forgot that it makes me puke."

There was a soft knock on the door, and Theodore showed his ID to the employee and took the new key card. He smiled at me, but it was more of a grimace. "Thanks, man. Sorry for barging in. See you at gala practice. I'll try not to be too hungover." He waved and was gone.

His suit jacket remained where I'd hung it

properly over the chair. I folded it over my arm and opened the door, but the hallway was already empty. His room must have been close by.

Suddenly, I wished I knew the number so I could return his jacket and give him the water. Did he have toothpaste and a toothbrush? Surely he did. I had Listerine, and it would help to gargle with it to get the acid aftertaste out of his mouth.

I considered knocking on every door on the floor until I found him, but eventually retreated into my room. I pulled off the coverlet, putting it on the spare bed. I discovered Theodore's tie crumpled on the tile floor in the bathroom and ironed it before carefully rolling it into the pocket of his jacket.

Read Henry and Theo's swoony romance in *Kiss and Cry*!

About the Author

Keira aims for the perfect mix of character, plot, and heat in her M/M romances. She writes everything from swashbuckling pirates to heart-warming holiday escapism. Her fave tropes are enemies to lovers, age gaps, forced proximity, and passionate virgins. Although she loves delicious angst along the way, Keira guarantees happy endings!

Discover more at:

www.keiraandrews.com